THE HOLY CITY

PATRICK McCABE

B L O O M S B U R Y
LONDON · BERLIN · NEW YORK

First published in Great Britain 2009
This paperback edition published in 2010

Copyright © 2009 by Patrick McCabe

Extracts from *A Portrait of the Artist as a Young Man* by James Joyce are
reproduced by kind permission of the Estate of James Joyce

Bloomsbury Publishing Plc, 36 Soho Square, London W1D 3QY

A CIP catalogue record for this book is available from the British Library

ISBN 978 1 4088 0075 1
10 9 8 7 6 5 4 3 2 1

Typeset by Hewer Text UK Ltd, Edinburgh
Printed in Great Britain by Clays Ltd, St Ives plc.

1 C.J. Pops, International Celeb

Now entering upon one's sixty-seventh year, one is at pains to recall such a blissful degree of contentment – ever. Welcome to the Happy Club, where our good fortune and well-being continue apace. Further enhancing the union of the lovely Vesna and her dutiful, respectful and ever-appreciative spouse: yours truly, Chris J. McCool – at your service, just call me Pops.

It has been remarked, of late, I have not failed to notice, how well I tend to look for my age – and in spite of a recent hip replacement too, I might add, necessitating the use of a walking cane. *Dashing* is a word which has – and not so infrequently, either – been generously and spontaneously applied. Such good-natured appreciations of one's status encouraging me daily to disport myself, as of old, in the smartest of neat blue blazers with brightly polished brass buttons, complete with white loafers and razor-creased grey slacks, a Peter Stuyvesant King Size cigarette (*the international passport to smoking pleasure!*) louchely dawdling between my lips. Completing the image – kinky, Pops, if that's your bag! – with just the teeniest sprinkling of Monte Carlo Man – the most expensive aftershave available on the market. I jest – there being no such fragrance in existence, of course. Old Spice, as ever, sufficing admirably, liberally sprinkled across the lantern jaw of 'retired businessman' Christopher J. McCool – 'Cullymore citizen', and refined boulevardier of some local distinction.

In passing, perhaps flippantly, there has been the somewhat flattering suggestion, tall and handsome as I am considered to be, of a more than passing resemblance to a certain Roger Moore, the cool, suave, unflappable star of stage and cinema screen. Who is perhaps best remembered for his portrayal of Simon Templar, the Saint, a self-styled 'jet-setting, country club' schmoozer very popular on television in the mid- to late-sixties. And that, of course, in later years, of that other post-war icon, the extremely sophisticated Mr James 'Licence to Kill' Bond, Ian Fleming's similarly enduring creation. A piece of intelligence which, were he to have become acquainted with it, my dearest old papa would, I feel confident, have found immensely gratifying. Dr Thornton being something of a sophisticated gentleman himself, of course – bred of the noblest, verifiably Protestant stock.

With his eighteenth-century Palladian-style mansion set in its sumptuous, painstakingly maintained grounds, boasting many priceless works of art, a 'capital' stables, and an absurd number of capacious and magnificently appointed rooms. Not to mention the extensive wainscoted library, with so many leather-bound spines glinting in the amber firelight, Father being something of a literary critic and essayist in his own right. Amongst those bookish treasures some of the world's finest works of literature. Most notably, perhaps, those of James Joyce, including both *Dubliners* and *A Portrait of the Artist as a Young Man*. A volume of which, in later years, for a variety of reasons, I was to become excessively, even – dare I say it – obsessively, fond. How proud he would have been of my artistic inclinations.

They could possibly have influenced him, who can tell? To the extent that he might even have come to regard me as a perfectly reasonable and valid human being. Not to mention his son and heir. Sired though I was at the back of a barn, by a representative of that most despicable breed, which he loathed with all his being, and routinely defined as 'Catholic scum'.

2   Abide With Me

In recent times, reinvigorated here in the modest quietude of the Happy Club, I have made it my business assiduously to proceed with the redecoration of our fine fourth-floor apartment. My latest purchases including a delightfully ornate Moroccan carpet, which I sourced on the web, and a Peter Blake print of the singer Alma Cogan – which, can you believe it, I actually found here in Cullymore East, in a little antique shop located along the Plaza. Also the loveliest low mahogany table, complete with polished inlaid chessboard. With which I like to amuse myself for protracted periods – whenever I'm not listening to Andy Williams or the Carpenters, one of their songs in particular seeming to provide the soundtrack to our new life.

– *We've only just begun,* sings Karen in that warm, mesmerising, melted-caramel voice, as I ease my head on to the comforting slopes of my beloved Vesna's bosom, drawing languidly on my Peter Stuyvesant, staring dreamily out at the stars.

– *Can't take my eyes off you,* croons Andy, as Vesna smiles and I run my fingers through her hair, kissing her frail shoulders, all along her pale freckled arm, as I whisper in her ear:

– In love's holy city we dwell. For me, my love, you will never be just a corpse.

We tend to retire early now, as a rule, and I can think of no greater comfort than the two of us just lying here, in that easeful silence we have signally made our own. With Vesna looking as delectable as ever, her helmet of hair gleaming platinum in the light. What with her Dreamland nightdress and Max Factor make-up, she almost makes the perfect model. Every inch as striking as Grace Kelly, say, or the remote but elegant Kim Novak in Hitchcock's *Vertigo*. Which has always been a favourite of mine. We rarely even bother going out any more. *Domestic bliss* – our very own club.

– *To sir with love*, continues Lulu – with another of our special 'mellow mood' favourites.

As I turn down the lights in our Happy Club home, fondly nibbling her ear as I lean in and whisper:

– Night, Vesna.

– Night night, Christopher. Chris my dearest, debonair darling.

Although, obviously, she doesn't use the word 'debonair'. For Vesna, poor thing, she can barely speak English. As, sifting her fair hair lovingly through my fingers:

– *Je t'aime*, I sigh, in my Serge Gainsbourg accent, as once more our flesh becomes one, a salutary, defiant celebration of love, that obstinately enduring, quite indomitable city. The most sacred place on Jesus God's green earth. And I should know for it's there I abide each and every single night.

– *The holy city*, I whimper anew.

As I crush my eager lips to her so-called 'dead' lips.

Whenever I do actually bother going down to the pub, which is situated just beyond the Plaza, I always endeavour to look my best, as if nothing is wrong or out of the ordinary – for I don't want anyone getting the wrong idea. And if they ever do actually enquire after Vesna and her welfare, I will always supply the usual excuse – that she's gone to visit her mother in Dubrovnik.

In the days before her quite appalling transgression – she committed adultery, I'm afraid I have to say – there were times when we would have gone out, why at the very least three times a week.

– Chris darlink, I is ready in moment, you would hear her say.

– Tsssssk, or – About bloody time! I would reply, as off we trotted hand in hand across the Plaza, on our way yet again to engage in a little 'swinging' – to 'get with' the 'fab' Mood Indigo beat.

Which of course has been cleverly targeted at us, the 'baby boomers', as we're called. Who, with our surplus cash and steadfast refusal to accept the passage of time are the perfect customers. Snapping our fingers as we bop till we drop, our hair turning silver like our hero Burt Bacharach. Yes, that's us: we're the 'groovy cats', the 'in crowd' of old. Yes, there they go, with their beads 'n' blue jeans – it's Pops and the Group – doing the Watusi out under the stars.

Not that there was much Watusi-ing going on in the little town where I happened to grow up. Indeed, to be honest, the only one who approached the status of trendsetter in the small and quite unremarkable village known as Cullymore was a rambunctious scallywag I happened to know at school, an eccentric, free-spirited individual who went by the name of Teddy 'the Hippy' Maher. Teddy had lived in America for a while and he was obsessed with California and 'the Summer of Love'.

– I'm telling you, Christy my man, he used to say to me, it's all happening out there. It's a revolution, buddy – there's no other word. It's crazy, Chris! Soon as I get my shit together, I'm heading right back – back to Haight-Ashbury and the groove!

It was around the time that Teddy did actually go back that I purchased my first ensemble of Carnaby Street-style 'gear', a blouson-style shirt, a psychedelic matching-collar-and-tie paisley affair in swirling pink. Yeah, crazy, groove – thangs! I used to repeat in what I perceived to be a fashionable American drawl, flamboyantly parading in front of the bedroom mirror.

But, lest I digress, let me return to my subject and share with you some facts about the club, Mood Indigo, this blue-lit, glass-walled theatre of musical delights to which I repeatedly, approvingly refer. In its heyday, there really and truly was nothing to compare with it. It was absolutely fantastic, it really was, and it's no wonder we'd look forward to it. I liked nothing better in those early days than getting myself

7

spruced up and heading out that door, clasping the hand of my 'foreign chic' girlfriend (think Elke Sommer, think Daliah Lavi), the sophisticated, statuesque, stunning-looking Vesna.

How I used to look forward to watching her getting ready. Being so particular about her appearance, she could spend an absolute age at it – dolling and prettying herself up even more, tugging on her crocheted mini or slipping into a chequered A-line dress. Her hair – as always (more Kim than Elke or Daliah, really) – piled up in that awesome, lacquered, great blonde tower.

Sometimes – just for fun – she'd incorporate this little dance she'd invented into the process, wiggling her fingers as she crooned Lulu or maybe Clodagh Rodgers. Both of whom we loved twisting to on the flashing multicoloured Mood Indigo floor. After a daiquiri or a couple of man-hattans.

– *Come back and shake me, take me in your arms!* I'd shimmy. As Vesna, for her part, did her best to emulate the diminutive redheaded soul crooner from Glasgow, shaking her hips – it was quite hysterical! – as she sang:

– *My heart goes boom bank a bank when you is near!*

About as far from Lulu's voice, I used to think, as the village of Cullymore was from the war-torn streets of suffering old Croatia.

One night we arrived at the club, Pops the Groover with his 'chick' on his arm, to find that the MC, my old pal Mike, was already more than halfway through his set. As usual, of course, as soon as he saw us coming through the door, he launched straight away into his absurdly daft version of a random Beatles medley. With 'I Am the Walrus' delivered, as usual, in his own inimitable style. That cleft palate of his, it really was hilarious:

– *I am the Eggmah!* he bawled, wrenching notes from the guitar as he grimaced. *I am the Walnut!*

– What a character, I said to Vesna, as we took our usual seat by the window.

– Whisky and soda, I requested, snapping my fingers, and the lady I think will have a margarita.

– Certainly, sir, yes of course, sir. Very nice to see you again, Mr McCool.

– Just call me Pops, I beamed, C.J. Pops, international playboy, ha ha.

When I knew Mike Corcoran back in St Catherine's, I have to say that really for me he was a kind of lifeline. He used to have me in stitches, with no end of cracks, crazy quips and daft sayings. Mike Martinez he calls himself now, and his stage outfit has to be seen to be believed.

– You gotta stay one step ahead of the punters, Pops, he'll tell me.

Direct from Vegas, his poster reads, and with that ludicrous fake tan he sure looks the part. Dripping in gold, with the sweat running off him, more than anything what he suggests is the fatal offspring of Julio Iglesias and Engelbert Humperdinck. But he's not bothered. Nope, as far as old Mike Martinez is concerned, no one in showbiz even comes close to him and his combo. So night after night, there's no stopping old Mike, shaking those maracas and doing the cha-cha like there's no tomorrow, as the bright and breezy xylophone chimes. While he shakes his hips and does the bossa nova. Schmoozing, as always, for the ladies.

– Yes, it's lounge! It's hi-fidelity! It's soft, it's lush but more than anything, it flows – we're the Chordettes, ladies and gentlemen. Welcome tonight to the world of Mood Indigo. Enjoy!

Like Mike always used to say – laughter is your friend: the crutch that enables you, against the odds, to make it through. And it's great to have that, really it is. For one thing I would hate is in any way to sound at all bitter about my upbringing. What purchase could there possibly be in that? And I don't want to end up blaming poor old Henry Thornton either.

It was just his attitude – that had always been the Protestant way. Henry Thornton prided himself more than anything on his aristocratic lineage and ascendancy heritage. And the time-honoured qualities they had instilled in him. Which he had described in his books as that 'sovereign, autonomous, self-contained ego formation against all possible incursions or admixtures, endogenous or exogenous'. The muscular Protestant character, he insisted, must at all times be secured against both its own passions and the invasions of others. For Henry Thornton, the ethos of uncompromising, hard-headed, rational self-interest could only serve to advance this imperative. Consequently, to him, all Catholics were to be apprehended as both unreasonable and quite hysterical – as the creatures of their own effeminate imaginations, the banshees.

How he must have reacted to the penetration of his wife by 'one of them' can only be imagined. Not to mention the fact that issue had succeeded their vile congress in the barn that night. In the final analysis, he informed her if she ever so much as looked in my direction, or associated my despicable existence 'in any way' with the big house, she would end up disgraced. She would die on the road like her peasant Fenian friends during the famine.

As regards my mother's furtive nocturnal visits to the little farmhouse where I grew up, I cannot say I remember a great deal. Except that they were welcome and pleasant, shrouded as they were in a kind of exotic mystery. It seemed to me, as a small boy, that she and her female companion came from a world wholly alien, albeit quite beautiful. One that was fragrant and all their own. One where elegance and 'ladylike poise' were prized above all else.

They wore gloves and tweed skirts and strings of pure white pearls. They spoke in accents with cut-glass vowels, which had clearly originated far from Cullymore, perhaps in London or the Home Counties of England. The mild-mannered companion, whose name was Ethel Baird, seemed remote in her eccentric attire – a veiled pillbox hat and what she habitually referred to as 'overshoes' – expressly purchased for her visits to the Nook, which was what they called the farmhouse, and which was located at the far end of the estate, across three muddied and thistled

11

rough fields. Where Wee Dimpie McCool, my guardian, took the place of my mother – and who often wept on their departure, I remember.

It was Ethel Baird, in fact, who had given me the book – my golden treasury, a volume of Robert Louis Stevenson rhymes. On a day long ago in the year 1950.

– This is for you, I recall her saying softly, as she carefully, patiently and methodically turned the pages, showing me the delicate illustrations of the constellations: those fantailing sprays of glittering diamonds that adorned the gleaming night-blue cover.

Ethel and my birth mother had been friends all their lives. They were fond of Wee Dimpie but would never consort with her socially – they couldn't.

Orthodox Protestant ladies – high-bred and discreet.

Obviously it would have been better to have a proper mother like anyone else but Wee Dimpie was a rock, in the circumstances, I have to say. There is not a bad word I could say about the woman. And she never tried hiding things, or telling me any lies.

– So that's who she was, I used to say when I got older, that's who she was – the 'mystery' lady! With her airs and graces and presents and food. My my! My own mother!

No, no 'mammy' on earth could have tended to my needs any better than Dimpie. Why, her breakfasts alone were enough to feed an army.

– Me auld pal Chrishty! she used to say to me. That took his name after the besht auld saint of all!

– She's Lady Thornton, isn't she, my mother? She's the wife of Henry Thornton of the Manor. Isn't she, Dimpie? Please tell me the truth.

– Yes, she'd say then, shuffling off with a bucket, scratching her backside as she wiped her mouth and shouted 'Chawk chuck chuck!', a scatter of red hens charging raucously across the yard.

Dympna McCool, it has to be said, was fond of me too, if in a functional, dutiful sort of way: she didn't pass all that much heed on me, to tell the truth. Generally being too busy haring off up to the chapel. For Wee Dimpie, I'm afraid, was a bit of a religious zealot, bestowing on me, as a consequence, the names of two of her favourite saints. St Christopher, to whom she declared she had a 'special devotion', and John of the Cross, he for no other reason that I am aware of apart from the fact that his fly-specked picture adorned the wall. But they were names, I suppose, as good as any other. So all in all, Wee Dimpie did her job well. Being big-hearted and nice in a kind of vacant, uninterested manner.

One thing for which I remain in her debt – she taught me all there was to know about rustic living. With the result that, by the time I was twelve years old – and it's amusing when you think about it, considering the cosmopolitan lifestyle I ended up embracing – there was very little about chickens and cow shit that C.J. Pops didn't know. As the two of us whacked the fat arses of Friesians, whistling as we trod the churned mud of the estate, Dimpie fingering her beads as she implored God for yet another batch of favours, before wielding her ashplant and bawling at the livestock:

– Will youse shoo outa dat, youse eejity bastards!

The Nook was nice and warm and cosy and it could have been a worse arrangement, I suppose. And one which, surprisingly without a doubt, had been facilitated, in a quite extraordinarily uncharacteristic burst of largesse, by Henry Thornton himself. Primarily, of course, to prevent the impending nervous collapse of my mother. The conditions he outlined were as follows:

– McCool can look after him down in the Nook. Just make sure he never darkens the door of this house, never once sets his foot across our threshold. Don't ever even dare bring him inside the gates. For, if you do, if you even consider it, my dear: be assured of this, you'll lose everything, all entitlements, everything that might be due to you. I'll see you walk the roads of this county for the humiliation that bastard Carberry has visited upon me.

After the passing of Wee Dimpie, God rest her soul – she died of cancer when I was in my late teens – I was subsequently informed by a solicitor that my tenancy of the house remained valid until I had attained the age of twenty-one. After which I would be expected to vacate the premises in order that ownership might succeed to the Thornton family. But, as it happened, poor old Henry went and passed away himself, not so very long after my mother in fact, and quite suddenly, precipitating some complicated wranglings in the family over

14

the will. So in the event, to my surprise but immense pleasure, no one ever did expel me from the Nook. And, as they say, between hopping and trotting, I was eventually informed that my tenancy was secure, provided I paid a nominal rent. With the result that, by the time adulthood had come around, lo and behold I was still lord of my little manor. King of my cottage and three acres of scrubland, with a dozen sprightly bronze chickens standing guard.

As I say, chiefly as a result of Wee Dimpie's tutelage, I by no means disgraced myself in the world of rustic authenticity. Indeed proved every bit as competent a yokel as any of them. And became well integrated, setting myself up in a dairy business. Purchasing a nice little tractor and trailer, now to be seen jangling about with my porringers and churns, dispensing my milk to the thirsty of the province.

– There he goes, Cullymore's very own Eggman! Young McCool there. How are they hanging? Will you leave me in a dozen of your turnips? And I think I'll have a porringer of crame! they'd call out good-naturedly as I came phut-phutting by, in my sturdy Massey Ferguson 35 tractor and trailer.

– There he goes! they'd cry. Cullymore's finest Eggman!

For the most part, I have to say, my neighbours tended to be genial fellows. Carrying on with their lives like their fathers and mothers before them.

– Howya, Eggman! A grand day now! Sure it's great to see it and thank the Lord for it! they would call good-naturedly after my tractor as I passed.

15

But deep in my heart I knew that even if I wanted it to be the case I could never be like them. Knew instinctively from the furtive nocturnal visits I had received of old and from Dimpie's veiled intimations and general behaviour towards me that I was 'different'. And that part of me would always be Protestant. Which was why I continued to be fascinated by Thornton Manor. That once breath-taking eighteenth-century edifice, clad in ivy and set in beautiful woodland, which was now on its way to becoming a ruin. So many times I made it my business to go up there just to gaze fondly at its crumbling towers, its grim Gothic dourness already becoming history, like the hegemonic ascendancy world of Dr Henry Thornton, esteemed literary critic, landowner and espouser of the traditional 'values of empire'.

And there I'd stand, in absolute silence, mesmerised, staring through the high French windows. Thinking about 'Protestants', their traditions and their values. And how, once upon a time, if things had been different, I might have ended up being one of them. Now, however, being just an impotent witness, to a world now fast fading, if not already gone.

So that was hardly going to happen, was it?

I thought about it nearly all the time – not just occasionally, or maybe now and then. I couldn't stop thinking about it, to tell you the truth. About the mysterious, fragrant night-time lady who came with parcels of food for Dimpie, who arrived with Ethel Baird her companion like a strange figure from a book. But what a beautiful book, it seemed to me now: a storybook of dreams that made you feel good.

And I would see myself there then, standing outside the high French windows of Thornton Manor, with Lady Thornton kind of blurred inside – as she sang 'All People That on Earth Do Dwell', turning the pages of the dreambook she was perusing. Before smoothing her hair and leaving down the book, moving sideways to look out at me. Before saying:

– *It's you that I'll always love the most, not Tristram. Not Little Tristram, C.J.*

I had imagined Little Tristram – of course there was no son in existence named Tristram Thornton, 'little' or otherwise.

But he would always seem so real to me when I stood there thinking about him that at times I could scarcely bear to look through those windows. For I'd see him so vividly – Little Tristram sucking his thumb behind the rain-speckled glass as she whispered them softly into his ear, those beautiful words of Robert Louis Stevenson's 'Escape at Bedtime', taken from *A Child's Garden of Verses*:

> The lights from the parlour and kitchen shone out
> Through the blinds and the windows and bars;
> And high overhead and all moving about,
> There were thousands of millions of stars.

Dr Thornton's works were all available in the local library. He was a commentator, historian, literary critic and essayist: there was no end to his intellectual talents. One of his works

17

was on the cultural antagonisms of Catholics and Protestants. And in which he attested, again baldly and confidently, that Catholics were by far the weaker species and that Protestants were innately superior. Always remaining impartial and neutral, self-controlled, dignified at all times.

I would think of them at evening gathered around the fire in the drawing room of Thornton Manor, arranged in a circle with their hymnals open, Little Tristram's voice soaring like a lark's above all the others, lovingly appreciated by all:

> – Abide with me; fast falls the eventide;
> The darkness deepens; Lord with me abide.
> When other helpers fail, and comforts flee,
> Help of the helpless, O abide with me.

As the soothing shadows of the evening fire flickered.

– The Protestant mind is indifferent, I would hear the good doctor say, self-controlled and sober. Judicious and equable, it tends towards abstinence. The Catholic temperament, however, is quite the opposite. It is vitiated, debauched, and quite degraded. Essentially of inferior status, I'm afraid.

Even as a fully grown adult now, seeing myself standing once more on the porch beneath the dripping willow trees, shivering and trembling – outside those blurred high French windows, with rain coursing down my face as I tonelessly repeated, chafing my palm remorselessly with the tractor keys:

– Help of the helpless, O abide with me.

18

3 Jerusalem

It was in the late summer of 1969 that I myself was fated to perpetrate my own rather particular and individual transgression. Which is the reason I found myself standing alone at the counter of Bernie's Bar that evening – ominously regarded by a phalanx of glowering faces.

– Committer of blasphemy, I overheard one of them say, defiler.

– He's Thornton's bastard, all right – sure enough. At the end of the day, the Protestant in him came out. The cold-hearted bastard that he is shone through.

– Hell's not hot enough for him. Not for a bastard that'd do the like of that. Fuck Jerusalem and fuck all niggers.

– Fuck all niggers.

– Whatever he wrote that for.

– And him black himself – the black Protestant cunt. It just shows you, doesn't it? At the end of the day, they're all the same.

I was sure they'd say something about my visit to Ethel's. I was certain I had been seen going up to her house. But they made no reference to it, and gradually it became apparent that they knew nothing at all about it. Not yet at any rate.

Then they got on to the subject of young Evelyn Dooris. Implying darkly that I'd threatened her – which simply wasn't the case. I had better things to do than go upsetting thirteen-year-old girls. And I didn't blame Evelyn for any of what had happened, none of it. Indeed, I admired her – her childish sauciness, her individual ways.

She too lived in Wattles Lane, and had been associating with the Nigerian boy Marcus Otoyo for some years now – ever since both of them had attended primary school, in fact. Now they both attended Cullymore Secondary, and were in their second and first years respectively. Marcus Otoyo was well known in the town as an extremely promising, potentially brilliant scholar. I knew him well from visiting the house in Wattles Lane. A friend of mine, Dolores McCausland, had been lodging there, a Protestant lady who hailed from the North.

I suppose, right from the very beginning, I had always tended to feel a certain kinship with Marcus Otoyo, even though, in 1969, at twenty-four years of age, I was obviously much older. Partly, I suppose, on account of his equally 'morally dubious' parentage. With the licentious miscreant in his case, reputedly, being an anonymous sailor from Middlesbrough. Who had disappeared for ever after a single night of illicit passion. Marcus was tall for his age, and slim, with glossy tight curls of jet-black hair. He carried himself in a refined, almost haughty manner.

I went to the house in Wattles Lane regularly. The lodger Dolores, being a Protestant, was never to be seen without an expensive string of pearls, in this particular habit being exactly like my mother and her friend Ethel Baird. But in almost every other respect she tended to differ completely from them. Dolores, for example, was much more forthright in manner than they would ever have dared to be, and infinitely more audacious in her choice of attire. There were to be no green two-piece heavy tweeds for Miss Dolores McCausland.

Or Dolly Mixtures, as she came to be known.

– That Protestant doll, the strap, the brazen hussy.

Who not only drank gin and smoked slim panatellas – but actually sang and sometimes danced in public houses.

– Diana Dors, go back to Ballymena, sometimes you'd hear the younger women mutter.

But Dolly never noticed. Far too absorbed in her own loveliness to be bothered.

It was true that I had defaced the walls of the cathedral. It was a stupid thing to do, I had acknowledged that almost immediately – far too emotional and vulnerable by half, something Henry Thornton and his ilk would never have dreamed, in a million years, of doing. Something they would have despised. In fact, even the very thought of desecrating a Catholic church was an action to which they would never have given a moment's consideration. From their point of view it simply wouldn't be worth it. Absolute indifference being their preferred weapon of choice. And which would, as it had been throughout history, prove infinitely more powerful in the long run. But then Henry and his like – they didn't know people like Marcus Otoyo.

21

People to whom indifference simply wasn't an option, however regrettable that might prove to be.

Marcus and Evelyn, as children growing up together, had over the years devoted themselves to the conversion of a disused greenhouse, along the railway track – about a mile from the town. And, quite impressively, had succeeded in turning it into a little place of 'retreat', I suppose you might call it. Viewing themselves as some kind of 'chosen' couple: a pair of saints, a brace of angelic oblates – but in a disarmingly innocent kind of way.

They used to go there every day – had been doing so ever since their earliest days in primary school. Mooning about the streets with their prayer books, as if to say: Us? Why, I'm afraid we're not of this world.

The only reason I had bothered going out to the greenhouse that day was to sort out the stupid contretemps between Marcus and myself. A stupid, embarrassing misunderstanding that ought never to have happened. I just wanted to explain my side of the story.

Receiving quite a shock when I discovered he wasn't there.

It was well after midnight and I must have been sleeping for three or four hours in the Nook when, tossing and turning, I heard the visitors arriving outside. First someone stumbling, followed by a mutter and a half-muffled grunt. I heard twigs cracking and then saw a long white face peering in the window – for all the world like melted wax in the gloom.

Canon Burgess had accompanied them, as it happened, providing, I suppose, the requisite moral authority. One of them struck me forcibly with a crooked stick. I don't know which one. All their faces remained a blur. When I looked again another priest had appeared: a small stooped fellow carrying a bible, muttering hesitant incantations. One of them was carrying a piece of the broken statue – I think it was Martin de Porres' ankle. Whatever he intended to do with that. Maybe because of saliva – I had spat a number of times into the saint's face – I guess they had assumed I had been 'influenced', that there were demons within me, or some such nonsense. Inhabited by Lucifer himself, I shouldn't wonder.

The police arrived at eight o'clock the following morning, asking a variety of questions about Ethel Baird.

– Of course I knew her, I told them honestly, a beautiful lady, refined to the last. She used to come to the Nook with my mother. She was like a countess you might see in a book. Always wore this veiled pillbox hat.

– Never mind what she wore. What were you doing up at her house?

– I wanted her to sing me a hymn, I told them.

Which was the truth. As I further explained:

– 'Abide With Me', as a matter of fact. And as soon as she did that, off I went about my business. I just took my book and said my goodbyes.

– You took your book?

– Yes, I took my book.

The detective went pale.

– You took your book and left the poor woman lying on the kitchen floor?

He turned to look at one of the officers. Who was suitably grim-faced as well.

– Are you aware you left her dying? That she almost died of a cardiac arrest? And that only for her neighbour, that's exactly what would have happened.

I said nothing, just stared over blankly at the fellow holding the piece of black ankle in his hand, who returned me an absolutely murderous glare.

4 A Child's Garden of Verses

It all seems so distant now, rendered even more remote by the quite extraordinary changes that have taken place in Ireland over the past number of decades. In so many ways, it's like a different country now. Why, even the Mood Indigo Club, in spite of its best efforts, can still never quite succeed in convincingly capturing the authentic feel of the sixties. Which was such a powerful decade culturally that it had even left its mark on poor old sleepy little Cullymore. With myself, now in my mid-twenties, doing my best to bag the prize, the honorary title of what I guess you might call the 'hippest mover' in Cullymore town. Yeah, Christopher J., dig him, chicks, for swingsville's where you'll find 'that cat'.

I used to pass the converted greenhouse every day. Above the door Marcus had nailed a little painted wooden sign. It read: *Enter ye here the Holy of Holies*. There were stacks of lavender blooms piled up inside and stretched across the glass panes a montage of pictures of assorted saints and mystics: a rosary had been hung around the neck of a statue. They would often spend entire Saturdays there.

I suppose I had become fascinated by Marcus's *blackness* more than anything. He looked so – *extraordinary*! And yet so calm and composed and self-reliant with it. So self-assured, or so it seemed. Exhibiting those very qualities which were supposed, exclusively, to define 'the Protestant'.

How had a black boy succeeded in managing that, I would find myself wondering. It had come to fascinate me, really, and I can't tell you how I admired him for it. A boy you'd have expected to be even more consumed by shame than the worst Catholic. A nigger boy, for heaven's sake. Even lower than the dog. That was what you were told. That's what you read. That was the way it was supposed to be. And yet here he was – acting like he was Prince of the Town. What a wonder, I thought. A miracle, of sorts.

Their singular devoutness began to exert the most peculiar and powerful effect on me. It could make me feel so vulnerable – at times close to tears. Whenever I listened to the two of them praying, the last thing I found myself wanting to be now was a Protestant. I didn't care how refined Protestants were, how wealthy or rational or self-reliant or disciplined or anything else they were. This had begun to seem a far greater mystery. I could have listened all to the hum of their young voices: I was hypnotised.

– Let's be Catholics, I would imagine myself saying, in the drawing room, to Lady Thornton, for it's softer and kinder. Much more tender. Mother, do you think we can?

And then, happily, I'd see her – Lady Thornton, one's Catholic mother, who would now so gladly take me on to her lap, turning the pages of *A Child's Garden of Verses* as she read in whispers from Robert Louis Stevenson.

– Do you like them, Christopher, my precious little Catholic boy? Do you like the stars? Why, you're a hundred times better than Little Tristram, that silly boy. I only read to silly Tristram because you aren't there. I only kiss him because I haven't got you. It's you I want to abide with, Little Christopher. You, my boy, and no one else. Sit up here in my lap and give Mama a kiss. Give Lady Thornton, your loving mama, a Catholic kiss. Human and giving, not hard and cold.

– I'm a Catholic, Ma, I'd say, amn't I? I'd say 'amn't I?' the way the Catholic children in Wattles Lane had always said it.

Before Lady Thornton would smile and sleepily nod, as the leaves of the volume turned and slowly fell.

5 Suits Me, Mrs Vindaloo

Down in Mood Indigo, in these the heady days of the relentlessly advancing noughties, a lot of the faces you'll see are black. Once upon a time, and I freely admit it, I might have had certain problems with that. After all, when all's said and done, what was Chris McCool way back then, only an ordinary old Irish dairy farmer, a country Eggman, whatever grandiose claims he might make for himself. And in that I was just the same as everyone else. Hayseed hillbillies who scarcely knew where London was, not to mention Paris or NY.

But that's all changed. That era's vanished. Gone for ever like so much of the world to which such facile attitudes belonged. Utterly transformed. Yes, the world has come to our door with a roar. Now you can do pretty much as you please, even mope about with a head like a balloon.

– Like a fucking balloon, Vesna Krapotnik – look, don't you see? They're all around us!

I remember the first day I made that remark. Vesna, I swear, nearly choked on her salad. Not that it occurred to me there had been anything particularly amusing about the observation. Not as far as I was concerned. It was just an aside, a throwaway statement. As far as I was concerned, all I was doing was stating the obvious.

– Let us welcome then, Vesna, the people without feelings. Who exist to consume, with their heads like ghostly moons, here in this twenty-first-century world of wax.

The first time I became aware of this extremely sly and subtle transformation of our surroundings occurred one otherwise perfectly ordinary day in September 2006 when I happened to be observing a few people eating dinner, as they say, al fresco, on the Plaza across from our apartment building. There was nothing, otherwise, unusual about this particular family I happened to be observing. They were simply relaxing, under an awning, consuming wine and eating pasta. An average family, complete with two or three children: all of them with perfectly rounded powder-white heads. Like puddings.

– The Balloon Family, I remarked to Vesna.

But not just ordinary ballons, I explained. Ones which were almost, without exception, utterly featureless – perfectly polished, smooth and dove-white.

There was a light wind blowing at the time and I remember thinking: I hope that little boy's head continues to remain upon his shoulders. I would just be afraid it might detach itself and drift away with abandon on the breeze.

Which it didn't, fortunately.

And when I looked again, they were all in exactly the same positions as they had been before. With the mother,

29

who was sporting an orange tan and a blue baseball cap, turning to her husband. I remember being struck: no eyes, no mouth. Moons *en famille*. Aesthetically quite pleasing, though, I have to say, in their uniformity, almost perfectly choreographed as they raised their disc-heads in unison, regarding the screens directly above the Plaza, steadily rotating with an eerie kind of poetry.

You can imagine how such a spectacle might, initially, have tended to be somewhat discommoding – even startling. No longer, however. In a small way, even, it's become almost reassuring: as though it reminds one of how far we have come in this newly urbanised country – having at last left behind the quite unnecessary and infuriating self-defeating ingrown complexities that were so much a part of rural life in Cullymore: where, inferring slanders and conspiracies at every turn, faces seemed to alter almost by the second. Where each random gesture seemed freighted with immense significance, every glance a semaphore reflecting the labyrinthine, complex intensity of suppressed passions within.

Little innocent Cullymore, where everything seemed to twist and turn by the day, and where, at times in your life there, you would have willingly parted with all your earthly possessions for the privilege of being seated beside such a composed and unthreatening assembly. With their milky sphere-heads seemingly emptied of guile, all considerations of conspiracy and subterfuge consummately erased. Gazing whitely at the turning plasmas, which pause at intervals as though in compliance with the directions of some invisible conductor.

– The Balloon People, I laugh, and Vesna thinks it's funny too, with heads like Eucharistic hosts!

As regards our non-national friends who are to be seen now in substantial numbers in Mood Indigo, let me say this. Attitudes towards those who might be described as 'non-indigenous' have only softened in this country quite recently. We are much more sophisticated now, it is routinely attested, and will never again be using words such as 'nigger' or 'Baluba'. We have moved on. And surely it is laudable that such is the case. But some time ago, I am afraid, we knew very little, if anything, about such matters. We were, and surely this must be contritely acceded to, laughably unschooled and ill-informed. Perhaps indeed a trifle xeno-phobic, if the truth be told. This was the nature of the world in which I grew up – whether it appeals to me or whether it doesn't. And which I hope will provide some explanation, however insufficient, maybe provide some background to the reason I insulted my psychotherapist Meera Pandit and called her unwholesome names.

Not that Meera was what you'd call proper black – not really. Not 'full-blown' black, I mean to say. Not Nigerian, for example – ebony – black and shiny the way that Marcus Otoyo was. Gleaming and polished, in that shiny African way. No, Pandit, you see, was a Hindu, not from anywhere near Nigeria, or anywhere else in Africa for that matter. I think from somewhere out near Bangladesh. As a matter of fact, to be fair to old Meera, now that I think of her, she was like something that might have emerged from the sixties herself, with her scarves and her bangles and her flappy Birkenstock sandals.

– You stupid black fucker! was, in fact, what I had said. I can't even remember what she had said to me to pre-cipitate that reaction – what her actual question had been, I mean. But I know it had something to do with Ethel Baird. As a matter of fact, it was all she seemed to want to talk about. Ethel Baird, or 'the music teacher', as she preferred to call her.

– Yes, all of that is fine, Mr McCool, she would say, usually after I'd been rabbiting on for ages, but can we talk about the music teacher, please?

– What else can you say about her? I replied. She was liked by everyone, kept herself to herself all the time. Was regarded by everyone as the almost perfect Protestant. 'The quality', they called her. 'Dearest Ethel,' they'd say, 'is the quality.'

– The quality?

It soon became obvious that she didn't have a clue. Pandit was hopelessly out of her depth.

Nonetheless, I did my best to explain:

– Upper crust. Respected. Well-off, but not showy, you know, Meera?

Then she looks at me in this funny kind of way and changes the subject all of a sudden.

– Why did you go there after you'd been to the green-house?

– I wanted her to read to me, I said.

32

– Read to you?

– Yes, I said, read: and maybe sing a little hymn.

– Sing a – what? A hymn?

– Yes, I said, 'Abide With Me'.

– 'Abide With Me'?

Of course with the way she was looking at me I might have said it was 'Delaney's fucking Donkey' I'd wanted.

Then she said:

– Well then, Chris, is there anything else you'd like to say about that time? About the nineteen sixties: about how you were feeling, what you might have been expecting from life? And this boy that you mentioned, this Marcus Otoyo –

– Niggers, Meera, I said, they're all the same. You can't trust any of them. They're even worse than Catholics.

When I saw her reaction then, I had to interject immediately:

– Ha ha, Meera, that was just a joke! Marcus Otoyo was an excellent fellow! Absolutely nothing wrong with him at all!

She didn't make any response to this, just seemed kind of sullen before continuing on.

– Now, you say that in your village, this town you call Ballymore, is it?

– Cullymore, I corrected.

I was so irritated that, after all my efforts, in spite of all the patience I'd demonstrated, she'd gone and forgotten the town's name again. That was the third or fourth time she'd done it. It couldn't have been all that difficult to remember, I kept thinking. So now, I'm afraid, it was my turn to be sullen. I didn't say anything for quite a long time. I kind of felt too, mainly on account of the way she was staring at me, some kind of an implication that for purposes entirely my own I'd been withholding certain facts from her. Facts pertaining to Marcus Otoyo, in particular.

I decided to clear the air once and for all.

– Look here, Meera, I began – with admirable restraint, I would have to insist, in the circumstances. It seems to me that these are the verifiable facts. Yes, I admired Marcus quite a lot. Indeed, at times, I think I might have even wanted to *be* Marcus Otoyo. Certainly to be as saintly as him: to experience the same overpowering depth of emotion to which he had access. Share in that celestial otherworldly transcendence. Do you know what I mean? To experience that *aura*. Which one exudes when they say one's in love.

– In love? she said quizzically.

– Yes, in love, I said, abiding in that holiest of cities. The most ancient place: the city of the open heart. It's so sacred, Meera. The truest holiness of which we mortals are capable. That's what I meant by the 'new Jerusalem'.

Then I became aware of her hooded, sceptical eyes. But by now I didn't care. I was prepared to let her think whatever she wanted. To me, all that mattered now was the truth. And I knew the truth. Which was – that all I'd wanted was the opportunity to be admitted through those portals. In order to be bathed in the light of Marcus Otoyo's singular faith. To be touched by his fervour and his unique passion. That was all. I yearned to do that.

What I hadn't told Pandit was that around the time when I'd met Marcus first, I had actually begun to do a lot of reading myself, unintimidated by considerations of whether I might be qualified to do so or not – having, in fact, terminated my schooling some years previously. At exactly the same age Marcus was now – seventeen. And had gradually become fascinated by the manner in which certain authors could describe their secret inner worlds, analyse the depths of the most elusive and complex feelings.

Once, quite by chance, I had happened to overhear Marcus reading from one of his schoolbooks to a friend:

– *My soul is cast down. I feel disquieted – so helplessly alone.*

I had never experienced anything quite like it and its subsequent effect on me was enormous. As a direct result of it I found myself seeing him, in a sort of late-night reverie, after I'd returned from Bernie's public house – Marcus ascending into heaven, black as ebony and wrapped in a winding sheet white as snow, with an expression of beatific rapture on his face. And had awakened, trembling, with warm tears welling up in my eyes. How could someone harbour such depth of emotion? How was it possible to experience it and remain alive?

– Why did you do such a terrible thing in the church? Do you think, Christopher, maybe you can tell me?

Thankfully now, there was something more appealing about her tone.

– If only he had accepted the book, Meera, that's all. If only he'd taken it – accepted it as a token. Instead of –

– Instead of . . . ? she quizzed hesitantly.

– Instead of insulting me, little nigger bastard!

One thing I regret is that in the course of my conversations during those sessions with Meera Pandit I had ever bothered mentioning Lulu, had even so much as opened my mouth about the Glasgow singer. For it soon became plain as day that the poor psychotherapist, she hadn't the faintest idea who she was. But the fact of the matter is, the only reason that I had introduced Lulu at all into the conversation was because it had happened to be one of her songs which had been playing on a transistor that day outside the library when I'd unexpectedly encountered Marcus Otoyo, combing his curls as he stood in the library doorway.

– Who is this Lulu? Why do you talk about her? asked Pandit.

– Oh would you ever shut up! I found myself snapping – my patience, finally, at an end.

The red-haired baby-faced Scottish singer Lulu had been one of the brightest stars of that particular year. There would have been no one more popular in Cullymore at that time. Except, perhaps, the Beatles – or the Rolling Stones. It had been the most wonderful year in Ireland, I remember. With a great sense of optimism now evident across the land, new houses and factories springing up everywhere. As for myself, I was making very good money indeed, selling my produce directly now to the new supermarkets, in particular the Five Star. But then spending it, I have to say, almost as quickly as it came in, on records and big meals in the hotel, as well as attending weekend dances in the Mayflower Ballroom, now unashamedly the dapper dandy in my crushed-blue-velvet pants and frilly pink nylon shirt. The music in the Mayflower had stirred the town from its protracted slumber. The bands that played there arrived in colourful vans, hauling out guitars as they swaggered in sheepskin coats. There seemed to be a never-ending supply of these musical outfits, whose names included: the Real McCoy, the Miami, Billy Brown and the Freshmen and, occasionally, from England, the Tremeloes, maybe, or the Herd.

There was a spanking new monument in the middle of the square, honouring the founders of the nation who had made the advent of the sixties possible. And directly across the street there now stood a fabulous new building with a great neon board whose green lights flashed *Redemption Centre*, proudly inviting all customers inside to exchange their Green Shield trading stamps for any number of fancy goods and household appliances. Items which included: vacuum cleaners, toasters, lampshades, garden furniture. But, even more enticingly, a bright display of 'she-gear for she-girls', modelled by mannequins gleaming and glittering in a variety of beads and sequins. Exulting in their narcissism with their wet-look go-go boots and rakishly tilted, knitted jockey caps.

Marcus Otoyo had picked me up all wrong, I explained to Meera, and that really was all there was to it. The whole thing had been unfortunate, I told her. Just what had I been thinking, Meera, I asked her, offering a seventeen-year-old boy a stupid kids' book? Of course he was always going to think it inappropriate. How could it be otherwise?

– It's no wonder he sneered at me, really, I said. At his age I'm sure I'd probably have done exactly the same.

Long before this incident – it was the night George Best had scored his hat-trick against Benfica, securing the European Cup for Manchester United – I happened, quite by chance, to apprehend Marcus going past, just across from me on the far side of the street. He was unaccompanied. Making, I assumed, his way home from Benediction. With his eyes elevated, and the leather-bound missal, as always, securely tucked underneath his arm. He was wearing his green gold-braided secondary-school blazer. Striding along in that otherworldly way. As if *the glories of the Eucharist held his soul captive*.

I could scarcely stand as I watched him pass. Then he briefly stopped, having encountered a neighbour.

I had a pain in my chest as I overheard him saying plainly:

– I sincerely hope you'll be coming to the performance of our play in the cathedral. The title has already been selected. It will go by the name of *The Soul's Ascent: Saints You May Not Know*. Myself, I shall be playing the part of Blessed Martin de Porres.

When I looked again he was gone and my deep-seated confusion and flushed countenance unsettled me.

*   *   *

I went to the Mayflower Ballroom again that weekend. Tina & the Mexicans were playing but throughout the whole performance I didn't hear a single note. Nothing but the bludgeoning thump of the bass.

I went home early and tried to read but found it quite impossible. My most recent discovery was the work of James Joyce, a volume in particular that I had seen Marcus carrying beneath his arm on his way home from school. The prose, however, of *A Portrait* continued obstinately to swirl before my eyes, defying all comprehension, defeating each and every renewed assault.

It was approaching four o'clock when I switched on the radio – only to hear that the Beatles had shot straight in at number one, with the double 'A' side, 'Penny Lane' and 'Strawberry Fields'.

Of all the things about the psychotherapist Pandit, what annoyed me most was the way she kept pretending to understand Irish culture when she didn't know the first thing about it. How could she possibly have done, anyway, when you think about it? For a start she had done all her training in London, and obviously while she might have known one or two things about the capital city of Dublin and the names maybe of a couple of Irish poets and politicians, as regards the subtler aspects of things it soon became clear that she possessed little or no knowledge of any value. Her attempts at empathy – they really were laughable. Especially when she'd try to forge some kind of link between Cullymore and all these Indian villages she kept going on about.

– Ballymore, she said – she'd gone and done it again, got the name wrong. It sounds so much like this little village I knew in Bangladesh . . .

That was the last straw.

– Look here, Pandit, I said, I've just about had it with all this. So how about you and your Birkenstocks just take off and you can tell Dr Mukti I said that if you want to. How about you tell your fellow countryman that? Because the only reason I agreed to these sessions with you is because he specifically asked me to. As if there was something special about you.

– I think we conclude our session now, she said.

As I sank my hands in my pockets and shrugged.

– Suits me, Mrs Vindaloo.

6 An E-Type Jag

For a lot of people, even yet, the sixties tend to represent a magical, almost fairy-tale period of history. *The Ronettes, Ray Charles, Yuri Gagarin, I'm Backing Britain!* . . . There seems no end to its imaginative, hopelessly irresponsible, deliriously childish wonders.

Even myself, in spite of all that has happened, I can still locate in those years the fondest of remembrances, which I continue to treasure. Things were so completely different then – almost exotic, even in Cullymore.

In May 1969, I had bought myself a state-of-the-art Bush record player, which provided me with many wonderful hours of entertainment. There was nothing I liked better than lying there in my bedroom in the Nook, thinking to myself that now at long last we had found a way out, that the decade of the sixties was destined to be our escape route, the road to liberation from the likes of Dr Henry Thornton and his fading, disappearing, antediluvian world. With the iconic poster of *Sergeant Pepper* on my wall, I'd peruse the sleeves of my LPs over and over. I had the Turtles and the Yardbirds and the Troggs but, best of all, the Kinks.

Any new album that came out, I made it my business to purchase it directly. Things were going so well with the supermarkets that money at that time was no object at all. I filled the Nook with artefacts and curios. A black-and-white Raquel Welch poster with *You Only Live Twice* beside it, whorled in red just above the door, with 007 looking menacing but impossibly glamorous. Then there were all the clothes. It was like the Nook had been moved to Carnaby Street. I had begun to think of myself as a kind of Ray Davies. Ray, of course, used to play with the Kinks and I was fond of his dry English irony and did my best to imitate him. Even down to buying myself a candy-striped blazer.

And the ladies, of whom I have as yet spoken little, generally, I have to say, seemed to approve. Some of the female out-of-towners who came to the Mayflower said that they thought I might be from London. They couldn't believe it when they heard I was from Cullymore, they told me, becoming nervous and eager to please. They were always making excuses to come out to the cottage.

– Gosh, you have so many records.

I'd give them little presents, a badge or a brooch with a film star's picture – Terence Stamp or maybe David Hemmings. Then we'd dance to the Troggs or the Beatles or Amen Corner. I really do have the most affectionate memories of that time.

– It's the sixties, I guess, and the old world is dying! It's goodbye to the cold and formal Protestant ancient world, goodbye to Henry Thornton and all that crazy, outdated bullshit! I'd say.

Not that it made a lot of sense to my guests. Who just wanted to dance to Lulu and Clodagh Rodgers. Or anyone else I might care to put on.

– Real gone, I'd say, and it's kooksville, babe! And now it's time for some Herman's Hermits!

As we did the Watusi in and out of some chairs.

– *No milk today, my love has gone away!*

– Chris McCool, you're a crazy guy!

– Maybe I am, doll, but you – you're the mostest!

I hadn't been down to Wattles Lane for some weeks now – I was afraid to actually go near it, to be honest, such was the strength of the feelings I'd recently been discovering within myself. Looking back on it now, that was probably the single greatest mistake I had ever made – capitulating to those emotions in the way that I did and permitting myself to return to Marcus's house. Maybe I'd just been unlucky. If I hadn't had the misfortune to meet his mother in the Five Star that day. She had specifically invited me down, you see, and I'd been arguing with myself all of the previous night about it.

I mean I knew it was risky. But then I'd think: What difference does it make? He's an ordinary seventeen-year-old boy, for heaven's sake. One who just happens to have an interest in the higher things in life, like I do myself. We have

43

shared interests. That's it. That's all there is to it. It's as simple as that.

So I managed, I suppose, to talk my way out of it. Or into it, perhaps, to be more precise. I nearly choked then when I met him on the street. I had just been leaving in eggs to the supermarket and was coming out whistling when I saw him standing there, as the Beatles say. He was carrying his satchel of books and staring in the window of the Green Shield Stamp shop. That, in itself, was hardly an act of any great note and it was only when I became aware of the object of his attention that I reacted. For it was a lady's nightdress at which he was staring. One I'd noticed in that window before, extravagantly described as being *edged in black lace, shimmering in frosted ice-cream pink. Come to Dreamland,* the attached card read. *It's soft and it's wonderful. Where the most romantic of dreams begin.*

It seems difficult to believe that now – almost forty years later – I would, quite by chance, find the exact same item, on the internet. Yes, of all places, on the World Wide Web, locate that very same delicacy. And take the opportunity to present it proudly to my beloved Vesna. To her absolute delight, producing the box as we sat together hand in hand in the Happy Club, home of the Carpenters and sheer domestic bliss. She looked so delicious as I primped up her coiffure.

– Welcome to Dreamland, I said, as I kissed her.

But as I was saying about that nightdress and Marcus. What continued to bother me as I observed him outside the shop was – why is his preoccupation with it of any importance to me? Why should I be even remotely interested?

I turned the key in the tractor and, as the engine spurted into life, I found myself recalling a familiar phrase, a snatch I remembered from *A Portrait*: *A trembling seized him and his eyes grew dim, for there appeared no respite from his inconsolable ardour.*

The best method of allaying my roused emotions, I decided, somewhat childishly perhaps, would be to effect some means of distraction. So for that very reason I treated myself, purchasing a record and some smokes – Peter Stuyvesant was the brand I had begun to favour. I found I relaxed quite considerably after that. The single I'd bought was an upbeat novelty tune, one recently penned by Lennon and McCartney, but now performed by a group called the Marmalade, entitled 'Ob-La-Di, Ob-La-Da'.

Thereafter, fixing my grub in the quietude of the Nook, I was gradually returned to my former state of carefree buoyancy. It's the sixties, man, I kept telling myself, I was young, for heaven's sake, only just turned twenty-five. What did I care about plays or James Joyce? Or, come to that, impossibly religious Nigerian boys who went about the town in braided bottle-green blazers. And who were, in any case, probably most likely only going through a phase, as did so many young people of his age. And with regard to which I was eventually proved one hundred per cent correct. If only I had bothered to pay attention to myself.

But right at that very moment, as I prepared my Vesta beef curry in a saucepan, I simply did not care at all. Which was why I had taken the decision to go out on the town that very night. Yes, head off to the Good Times, which was opening later on. Cullymore's very own new 'swinging bar', complete with Rock-Ola jukebox and a stage. It was unique, and everyone in town was already singing its praises. So yes, I repeated, I would have to pop down and check out all the action. Schmooze all the talent and have a few beers.

It turned out to be fantastic, with a lot of chicks who'd been specially invited. We all really let our hair down that night.

– It's the new sensation! we laughed – but it was.

It was only going to be a matter of time before I bought myself a car. Which, by modern standards, was extremely humble, I'm afraid I have to say. A 'fab' Ford Cortina which I'd been looking at in the showrooms for some time. But I mean, let's face it – it was hardly ever going to be an E-Type Jag! Sure I was earning reasonable money – but I couldn't say I was Ronnie Kray yet! Two hundred quid I picked it up for. I might have been Lord Snowdon as I cruised the country roads in my frilled Ray Davies shirt.

Grooving with the ladies in the Mayflower and the Good Times.

– This is a grand new car that you've got.

– It sure is, baby, it's a real mean machine.

As onward we cruised and Cullymore's answer to Pattie Boyd snapped her fingers, pressing the transistor up against her ear, as we chanted along with 'Wild Thing' and the Troggs, the raw ragged metal guitars of '69 shining silver in the summer air.

7 A Very Clever Plan

Dr Mukti, Pandit's superior, was an Indian the very same as her.

– Fucking curry munchers, Mike Corcoran used to say, they're getting in everywhere. Pontificating to good men like you and me.

I'm afraid old Mike was a bit funny in that regard. But really, back then, everyone was. Except that Mike could take it a little far.

– Gas all the gypsies, you'd hear him saying on a regular basis. Set aside an afternoon and round the whole lot up. You'd be doing everyone a favour, Christy. And the nigger boys too – scoop a few of them.

Now, however, in these rehabilitated and reformed, more enlightened days, he doesn't give a damn about any of that. If he ever did. It was the drink that put him 'astray', he claims. And in point of fact, for most of our time in St Catherine's Psychiatric Hospital, he and Mukti got along quite well. To give Mukti his due, there were times when he could be something of a character himself.

– Don't talk to me about the bloody sixties, he could say.

Bunch of bloody children, isn't it! Most overrated generation ever the world has known!

Reluctant though I might be, I have to, in retrospect, acknowledge that there is a certain amount of that statement with which I would find myself inclined to agree. But only someone like Mukti would have had the courage to state something so baldly and directly. For that reason, he had always seemed kind of Protestant to me. Not initially, perhaps, but always ultimately admired for his steadfast adherence to principle: his grace under pressure. The muscular rationality of his approach. Mike Corcoran, as I say, secretly liked him too. As indeed he ought to, for the doctor had performed a near miracle on the man.

Poor old Mike. When he first came into St Catherine's, he really was in an awful state. I knew him, of course, from our days in Cullymore, where he'd worked as a musician with a small pick-up band. Like a lot of musicians – and he is regarded as one of the best: a multi-instrumentalist, who can literally play anything, he got himself into bad trouble with the bottle. To such an extent, in fact, that he ended up busking, without a penny, on the streets. In a truly dreadful way – scarcely knew his own name, to tell the truth. Until the eminent Dr Mukti, 'the Protestant', came along.

To give you an example of how bad Mike actually was: one day I happened to be sitting in the lounge minding my own business, just watching something stupidly inconsequential on the television. When, all of a sudden, he gets a hold of me round the neck and starts shouting:

– You fucking bastard, you screwed my wife! Why, Chris – why did you do it? We were friends!

The laugh being, of course, that the lunatic doesn't even have a wife!

But that's all over, as I say. Mukti cured him. Good old Mukti cured him completely.

– He's a genius. An absolute genius, Mike would often privately say, shaking his head in disbelief and gratitude.

Which was exactly the opinion I used to have myself. Before my eyes were opened – about so-called Dr Mukti. Who swore blind to me that Pandit had been transferred to another hospital and that he, personally, having 'cleared some space', would now be taking over my case. For a long time, I had actually believed him. But the whole thing turned out to be a clever little ruse – quite heartless, really – a wily conniving scheme to get me to talk. So much for Mukti the straight-talking honest Protestant. I couldn't believe it the night I saw Pandit. Through an upstairs window on the terrace. Quite by chance, late one summer's evening, tossing her head back as she laughed at some joke of his. Anyone looking would have assumed her and Mukti to be involved in some form of illicit affair. Whether they were or not didn't interest me. My only concern was their treachery and disregard for my feelings.

But I didn't say anything, made no reference at all to it. I kept my powder dry for about another fortnight or so – just to see what exactly was going on. I laid eyes on Pandit on no less than four occasions after that first time. Yes, Meera

Pandit, Mrs Vindaloo, who else, whom I'd been solemnly assured had long since 'left' the hospital. The implication being that, chiefly because of her failures with me, she had now been assigned to 'other duties'. It was flattering, obviously. But, unfortunately, however, was a complete pack of lies. A clever ploy by Mukti to get me to think well of him, to consider myself 'singled out' and 'special'.

Bollocks.

All Mukti seemed to want to do now, 'now that we are on an even keel again', was to start more talk about the sixties. Which I found rather strange, not surprisingly, having heard him disparage them so vehemently before. I withdrew resentfully once I began to realise what he was doing. Trying to relax me in order to get me to talk. That was the reason he was blabbering on. Ever so subtly then, when you weren't expecting it, returning to the subject of Marcus Otoyo. He kept on doing this and then smiling cloyingly, as he elaborated on that 'lunatic decade, the permissive sixties'.

– It was a time of great turbulence, wasn't it, Christopher? he blathered on, toying with his pen in his big padded leather chair. The Paris riots. Industrial unrest, the primacy of the individual and the beginning of the end of the concept of 'the common good'. This too is the legacy of the age of the Maharishi, of John, Paul, George and Ringo.

Then suddenly, again unexpectedly:

– Ah yes, Marcus Otoyo. Tell me about him, please.

I could see through it all so plainly now, and regretted any trust I had ever placed in him – any respect I had ever had for the man. In my eyes now, he was even worse than Meera Pandit. Now. His voice slowing down as he leaned across his desk.

– Tell me about them, Christopher, the sixties as you lived them in your little Irish home town.

I was way ahead of him, grinning from ear to ear.

– Yeah, the Beatles, man! I beamed – with a convincing, boyish enthusiasm.

But, in spite of myself, my eyes had begun to smart as I inwardly considered the potential enormity of this fresh betrayal.

– Marcus Otoyo. He returned to it again. With that chilling, self-serving, unctuous smile.

– Tell me, please.

Let me make it clear, however, that in no way do I perceive anything I might have apprised regarding the nefariousness of Mukti's wiles and deceptions to excuse what I did to him later on. My actions in that regard were wrong and unjustified, that's about all there is to it. If only I'd been capable of subordinating my will, not yielding before the tide of instinct and emotion. Of exercising rational judgement. But I didn't. I succumbed helplessly to my baser instincts, my weakest desires. One can only surmise what the reaction of Henry Thornton might have been.

– Loathsome. Infirm. Vitiated, degenerate. Lower than the dog.

8 Sand

Looking back on it all now, with the benefit of over twenty years of hindsight, as far as I'm concerned, after my treatment of Dr Mukti, I had more or less asked for everything that was coming to me. And deserved, as I duly was, to be carpeted – dumped, bag and baggage, into the spartan solitude of the White Room, within its fastidiously distempered walls there to be indefinitely detained. To become a bleached soul in a neutral enclosure. It was entirely appropriate.

Once I had found myself eating directly opposite Marcus Otoyo in Cafolla's Café on the main street of Cullymore. As usual he was wearing his blazer, sitting in the booth, casually reading as he dazedly combed his hair. Maybe if that had never happened – if I hadn't been there in Cafolla's that day, if I hadn't witnessed him flicking through those pages, I might never have begun to associate the book with him. Would never have made any connection at all. But there it was – *A Portrait*.

It was as if a hand was reaching into my soul – and I found myself yearning to know what particular section he was studying. At last I was presented with my opportunity when he vacated his booth to go to the toilet. He hadn't seen me. My heart was beating furiously as I lifted the volume, my eyes drawn immediately to the underlined passages:

> *A girl stood before him in midstream, alone and still, stood gazing out to sea: and when she felt his presence and the worship of his eyes her eyes turned to him in quiet sufferance of his gaze, without shame or wantonness. Long, long she suffered his gaze and then quietly withdrew her eyes from his and bent them towards the stream.*

I continued down the page, my heart still racing:

> *He climbed to the crest of the sandhill and gazed about him. Evening had fallen. A rim of the young moon cleft the pale waste of skyline, the rim of a silver hoop embedded in grey sand; and the tide was flowing in fast to the land with a low whisper of her waves, islanding a few last figures in distant pools.*

It would have been so much better if I had never in my life gone near that booth. For that night in the Nook I dreamt the whole thing so vividly – as we lay there together, islanded on the strand:

– She's beautiful, isn't she, Marcus? I said, casting a pebble across the blue canopy of the night.

– Yes, he replied, resting his chin on his hand as the waves broke upon the shingle.

– You were wonderful, you know, in the play. The town is so proud of you.

He leaned on his elbow, looking up at me and her as he smiled.

– It's the sixties, he said. Let's not talk about the town. This time next week we'll both be in San Francisco.

– San Francisco, I heard myself sigh, moving about the cottage, flushed and out of sorts – in a helpless daze.

Not even knowing I was smoking the cigarette until the record came to an end, crackling repeatedly until the metal arm eventually drew back, and Eric Burdon and the Animals began to recede. And with them the promise of those warm San Francisco nights, in that dirty old part of the city, as Eric had just sung, *where the sun refuse to shine.*

A promise fading, glimmering and diminishing: like a tiny light, as James Joyce had written, beyond a pier-head where a ship was about to enter. Almost out of sight, just like the girl who, very shortly before, had waded so breathtakingly into the water. With her skirts kilted boldly and dovetailing out behind her, her bosom as soft and slight as a bird's.

The Altonaires were playing in the Mayflower that weekend but their music was dull and I kept wanting to go home, all they kept playing were dreary old fifties novelty songs and in the end I left in the foulest of humours. The girl in whose company I found myself wasn't exceptionally pretty but she made it clear that she liked me a lot – which I have to say was flattering.

– I see you going about the town on your rounds, she told me, and I've often seen you above in Cafolla's.

I had no desire to offend her. She looked quite wonderful in her Tammy-style dress. But all I kept thinking of was the girl wading into the water and lying there with Marcus Otoyo, the two of us chatting away about poetry. About Robert Louis Stevenson and *A Portrait*, so contented, prostrate on the sand.

When I looked again, the Tammy girl was kneeling beside me, her cheeks colouring pink as she nervously enquired:

– Do you think you'll be going to the Mayflower next week? The Sands are playing there on Saturday.

Tony Kenny played with the Sands. I liked his music but I wasn't sure if I'd be going.

– I just don't know, I remember telling her. Maybe, I said. I really just don't know.

9 Any Views on That, Mahatma Gandhi?

There were a few things that consistently kept bothering me in the White Room. I couldn't stop wishing Stan Carberry hadn't interfered with my mother. I wished more than anything that he'd left her alone. Why did he have to go and do that – bring her out to the barn that night?

And I wished that I'd never known anything about religion – Catholic or Protestant. I wanted to know about neither. And yet at the same time I wanted to know everything. Why could I not be like everyone in the sixties, I kept asking myself, and say that God was dead: Hey, man, take it easy, no need to worry, nothing bothering us cats down here.

But more than anything what was bothering me was what I'd done to Mukti. It was wrong and I knew it. Except I also knew this: that, if I capitulated this time, not only to excessive feeling but to any kind of vulnerable emotion at all, my time in that White Room could prove to be devastating. Worse than anything I'd experienced so far. And I couldn't risk that.

In the sixties they said people kind of liked being a little mixed up. That was what the Beatles were always insisting: take, for example, *I am he as you are he* etc., from 'I Am the

Walnut' as Mike Corcoran sings. Or should I say Mike Martinez, ha ha, later of the famous Mood Indigo house band the Chordettes.

Yeah, that was the way. Identities were frivolously encouraged to fracture in those days, to turn themselves upside down and inside out, through the influence of drugs, alternative therapies and who knows what else. With nobody so much as batting an eyelid at any of it. No, it was all about getting your kicks, man. You could be everybody and nobody all at once. Nothing and everything all at the one time. It was 'thrillsville', they said, 'too much' and 'outasite'.

But it didn't turn out that way for me. I heard later from Mike that Mukti was supposed to have been heartbroken with the way things had turned out.

– Then he shouldn't have tried to trick me, should he? I said to Mike.

And what reply could there possibly be to that?

– It was just a pity, though, Chris. I mean – boiling water, for Christ's sake.

And I know it's true – and I deeply regret it, I genuinely do. Trickster or not, none of that ought to have been necessary with Dr Mukti.

I was kept in the White Room for quite a considerable period of time, don't ask me how long – I lost all track. Then one day, quite unexpectedly, when I was chewing my nail in the corner and thinking, to be honest, mainly about nothing, the most extraordinary thing happened. At the very first indication of that soft and faint, very measured tapping behind the ventilation grid I inclined my ear forward, my initial consideration being that it might be a small creature: a mouse, for example – or a timid little bird. And persisted in thinking that – excitedly, I have to say – as I inspected the serrated grid for a sign. An indication.

The curved whisker of a rodent, perhaps, I considered, or a small distended avian claw.

Then I heard another sound – this time different, soft but resolute nonetheless. It suggested a thin wooden panel sliding back sharply. Barely perceptible, but indisputably *real.* I started backwards in expectation, but, in fact, nothing happened. With nobody – or nothing – appearing for quite some time. It had all the hallmarks of some kind of subtle charade. Like someone was trying to 'take a hand out of you', as the old farmers used to say long ago. But then, after another short while this small brown hand, hardly even the size of a doll's, appears out of the ventilation grid, so positively, absurdly and quite ridiculously tiny that you could not help but be amused.

And before you could say anything at all, whose head appears – I could scarcely believe what I was seeing myself – none other than that of Dr Mukti himself, the noted head psychiatrist of St Catherine's Hospital. But a psychiatrist unlike any I had ever seen before – one who could not possibly have been more than six inches in height, handsomely attired in his buttoned-up Nehru-style jacket, a little blue cotton cap perched on his head like a boat. With some old ancient Hindu nonsense scribbled on it. He looked so content, almost blissfully so.

Which explained why, initially, I was on the verge of greeting him in that same familiar, almost affectionate manner we'd been accustomed to when we first met. Before hostilities opened up between us. But I was soon to be disabused of any such facile intentions.

For his expression already had grown grave and darkly formal. As he waved his finger and chastised me formidably for my recent undignified, unworthy behaviour. Repeating harshly:

— You're just about the rudest man I've ever known, Christopher John McCool. Saying those things to me that day in my office. Have I not at all times told you the truth? You cannot deny the fact that I have. Why then, don't you ask yourself, would I bother to go to the trouble of deceiving you in this instance? Can't you see it's your own innate weakness, your complete failure to put your trust in those who might be able to help you that has been causing you all these unfortunate problems? You really are your own worst enemy, McCool!

I knew now what he meant. And that, probably, in all likelihood, his accusations contained a lot of substance.

Apart from the bit about the Catholic priest, anyway. Which only served to show how little, just like Pandit, in spite of all his much-vaunted experience, he actually knew. And how hastily he himself tended to jump to conclusions and embrace stereotypes. He'd been labouring, it soon became clear, under the illusion I'd assumed his visitor that day – on the 'day of the boiling water', I suppose you might call it – had been a Catholic priest. And that it had been my supposed resentments towards this fellow, having grown up with my peculiar history in a 'small repressed Irish country town', which had prompted my actions. How uninformed can you possibly get.

When nothing, in fact, could have been further from the truth. I wasn't even remotely interested in his visitor, and I certainly bore no animosity towards him or his clerical colleagues, for any 'damage' inflicted on me, or anything else. There was only one reason why I had followed them into the kitchens that evening and it had nothing to do with visitors at all. It was Mukti I was after, Mr Clever Clogs Mukti, steering conversations to get people to catch themselves out, yes, Mr Entrapment Mukti – treacherous fucking Indian bastard!

Anyway, even at a distance you'd have had to've been blind to think it was a Catholic priest. For a start his suit was light charcoal grey, so although he was a clergyman, he had to be either Methodist or Church of Ireland – one or the other. In any case, as I say, that poor unfortunate fellow was irrelevant. He, unhappily, happened just to get in the way, and that's probably the thing I'm most regretful about of all.

But, anyway, as I say, 'little' Mukti went on blathering. Except with this laughably squeaky voice now – it made me double up every time he opened his mouth – ever so reasonably explaining it all to me, with his diminutive doll's hands gesturing as he did his best to sound intelligent. Not only had the clergyman not been a Catholic priest, he continued patronisingly, but he had come to St Catherine's to visit his brother, who was an alcoholic.

– An alcoholic? I choked – pretending to be concerned – deciding to play him at his own game. In fact, scarcely listening.

– Yes, he went on, an alcoholic with very severe problems indeed, every bit as bad as yours, Mr Christopher McCool. And I'm sure that his brother has a lot more to do than come around institutions looking out for his troubled relative without finding himself in mortal danger. Would you have anything in particular to say to that?

No I hadn't, I assured him. What could I possibly say, I said. It was disgraceful what I had done to them both – without question.

– I am deeply, Dr Mukti, deeply remorseful over what I did. I implore your forgiveness. I am abject, craven, ashamed of myself.

And that is exactly what I would have gone on saying if, quite unexpectedly, I hadn't seen him smirk. And cover his face with his cupped chocolate-coloured hand as he whispered:

– *Marcus Otoyo was right. You really are quite the freak, aren't you? But not in an amusing sixties kind of way. Oh no.*

I went cold all over as soon as I heard that, my muscles stiffening and the hairs on my neck beginning to bristle. Then I found myself responding bitterly.

– Excuse me, Dr Mukti: would you mind repeating what you said just now?

– Repeat it? he replied, provocatively confronting me.

I began to become aware that I had responded too eagerly. Small though he was, Mukti was still clever and had lost none of his dexterous artfulness. Already I could see the eager glint of perceived advantage in his eye.

– Yes, I said, repeat it, please, if you wouldn't mind.

His reprised smirk undermined me again. As did his suave and patient demeanour. The high-pitched tone had all but vanished now from his voice.

– You must be imagining things, Christopher, he said, because you see, I didn't say anything at all.

I had become extremely agitated now and was fumbling awkwardly, without success, for words.

Eventually I said:

– Well, vuh-vuh-very well, that's fine, but I'm sorry you did not, only that there was a smuh-smuh-smirk on your face when you were saying it.

Now he was making me stammer – something I did rarely, only when I was very upset.

– Saying what? he said then. Please tell me what I said. If you heard me saying something then please tell me what it was.

I couldn't stand it. I knew I had to do something. I snapped.

– Oh fuh-fuh-for God's sake, Dr Mukti! I bawled, with my voice now in a higher register than his. Will you stop this nonsense once and for all, for goodness' sake! I heard what you said! I know what you're trying to say – that my intentions towards Marcus Otoyo were somehow dishonourable and that all this talk of literature is just a smokescreen of some kind. Well, let me tell you something – how about you and that Pandit take off and go back home: back to India or wherever it is you came from! What do you think of that, Tom Thumb? Any views on that, Mahatma fucking Gandhi? Anything to say about that, have you, foxy? Well? Well? Wuh-wuh-well?

10   The Mysteries of Protestants

Thankfully, all of those minor little turbulences are well past now, long since over and consigned to the dustbin of history. And, like so many events throughout the course of my life, I am in the fortunate position of being capable now of recollecting them in an almost luxurious and sleepily random fashion – lying here on my soft velvet cushions in the Happy Club listening to my CDs of the Carpenters and Tony Bennett and all the others and thinking again about poor old Dr Mukti. Whose good points I can appreciate now without the slightest hint of rancour. As I can, in actual fact, with almost everyone I've known over the years, with whom I have been connected – Marcus Otoyo, happily, included. Whose poise and refinement, intelligence and erudition really were, by any standards, quite remarkable for their time. And in such a quiet, unprepossessing place. I can see how their uniqueness might have come to impress me in the way that they did. How in so many ways he came to embody the spirit of radiant, adolescent wonder itself – a spirituality and longing I could find nowhere else. And which was so perfectly described in the writings of James Joyce. Who belonged to no age in particular, and who infinitely, culturally and artistically, if one was honest, was superior to anything emerging from the narcissistic, throw-away, congratulatory, complacent and fly-by-night sixties.

I embraced every word that I found in *A Portrait*, surrendering to their 'passionate euphony'. And became convinced that Marcus Otoyo was a kindred spirit in this regard, that he had been thinking along those lines too. You could tell, I persuaded myself, by the way he carried himself: mysteriously detached, at one remove from the world in which he lived. Sometimes at night I would think of him praying: not in a remote, stark frigid Protestant cathedral but in a warm and big-hearted Catholic one, where the altar was heaped with fragrant masses of flowers, and where in the morning light the pale flames of the candles among the white flowers were clear and silent as his own soul.

I thought of him blinded by his tears and the light of God's mercifulness, all but bursting into hysterical weeping as he watched the warm calm rise and fall of the girl's breast that day on the strand. With the glowing image of the Eucharist uniting in an instant his bitter and despairing thoughts. While sacrificing hands upraised the chalice flowing to the brim. So far distant from the Gothic grey grimness of what was left of Thornton Manor. And the lives of all who had lived there: in a place which, beside this, was the colour of dust. The shade of the gravestone that was Henry Thornton's face. No, a book such as Robert Louis Stevenson's *A Child's Garden of Verses* meant nothing to him, not in any real human way. Maybe not in any way at all.

Yet another indication of Catholic sentiment: unreliable, quite despicable emotionalism.

One troubled night I dreamt of Henry Thornton, my eyes snapping open, still seeing him bursting dramatically through the high French windows of Thornton Manor, with rain and sheet lightning sweeping out behind him, his face a mask of bitter resentment, tearing the book *A Child's Garden of Verses* from Lady Thornton's pale trembling hands. Before casting it contemptuously into the roaring flames, its thin leaves edged in gold immediately turning to ash in the heavy grate. As I fled from her lap, out into the yawning black maw of the night – hopelessly blinded by bafflement and sorrow.

Resounding in my ears the mercilessness of his chastisements, as he continued to charge her with that most grievous sin.

– Fornicating with Carberry like a common fucking whore, and bringing that oddity, that thing into the world! You call yourself a Protestant? You think they'll ever show respect to you again? They'll despise you from now till the day you die, for showing weakness above all to one of them!

On the day of the 'boiling water', what happened was I had been following Mukti – more or less for the whole morning, in fact. Now, at close of evening, I found myself concealed behind the sundial, under cover of some bushes, eyeing him closely as he led his visitor in the direction of the prefab, where they held the group sessions, specifically for alcoholics.

I was feeling very cold – icy, to tell the truth – as I observed them chatting, ever so warmly, and smiling. What seemed so strange was that the feeling in its essence was so close to the one I remembered from long ago in Cullymore. After I'd discovered the letter of betrayal. The crumpled envelope I'd found in Dolores's handbag. Dolores McCausland and I had established a liaison of some significance at the beginning of summer in 1969, after a number of meetings in the Mayflower Ballroom. She was a woman some years older than myself, and her presence in Cullymore had literally electrified the town. The truth was that they had never seen anything like her before. An entirely different kind of Protestant, with her peroxide hair and figure-hugging dresses. They said she looked the 'spit' of Ruby Murray, a Northern Irish singer who'd been very successful some years previously. And whose songs she had declared a particular affection for, actually singing them in public from time to time. She was attracted to me, she said, because someone had told her I was a Protestant. I'm not, I told her, and did the best I could – but she wouldn't permit herself to be convinced. I heard you have associations with quality, she said – and laughed.

– We all stick together, she chuckled mischievously the first night I met her, because we're different to them! They can get themselves in such a tizzy about silly things, can't they, the Catholics? Like a little slap and tickle, for instance. Or a girl's fondness for a nice cheeky dress. They won't even allow the *News of the World* into the house! Kiddies, really, I sometimes think. They're so predictable but lovable in so many ways. They can have such fun with their singing, you know, and their drinking! Love them Fenians – bless 'em, or hate 'em – one way or another, you can't be without them!

But I'm really not a Protestant, I continued to insist to her. Meaning that part of me would, regrettably, remain for ever Carberry. And that was just about as Catholic as you could get. The inebriate, treacherous, unreliable rascal.

– I don't care what you say, she said, I can tell. The way you dress, even the way you walk. Yes, you're every inch the gentleman, she insisted, and that's why I shall christen you my own *Mr Wonderful*.

I really became fond of Dolores McCausland, the lovely 'Dolly'. Each weekend now I took her to the Mayflower and we would enjoy a drink most evenings in the Good Times. She liked the Beatles but preferred Peggy Lee.

– That's because she sings little songs about you, you see, she laughed, puckering her nose as she sipped her drink, crooning:

– *Why this feeling? Why this glow? Why the thrill when you say hello? Mr Wonderful, I love you!*

Whenever we had a disagreement she told me she didn't like me looking at her in that way.

– Don't do that, Mr Wonderful, she implored.

– I thought you liked Protestants, isn't that what you said?

– Not like that. Not all Protestants are cold and hard.

– The indifferent grey heart of Henry Thornton. What other kind of Protestant is there?

– Please don't shout, she said, it upsets me, I told you, when you look at me that way.

– OK, baby! I won't, after all it's the sixties and we're supposed to be 'real gone', in 'kooksville', having fun. So let's put on the Troggs, OK? Yeah – *Waaahld thang*! It's the new world, baby, roll over, Henry Thornton!

The light on the terrace was beginning to fail but the visitor and Mukti were still out front. When I looked again, though, they had disappeared around the side of the building. I followed them. They took a left turn past the prefab, indicating they intended to avail themselves of the available short cut, past the car park and then in through the kitchens. There was an open slatted door on rollers at the side of the building and through it came wafting the stultifying smell of pulped, boiling cauliflower.

The psychiatrist climbed up on to the concrete ledge and assisted his visitor, the two of them laughing as he climbed up and was hauled inside. I craned my neck but couldn't properly make out what they were saying.

There were some sacks of potatoes stacked up near the boiler, with two huge metal bins stuffed to the brim with soggy broken eggs, potato skins and other damp refuse. I slipped inside and didn't make a sound, crouching down out of sight behind the sacks. The two men had paused and were chatting amicably to the kitchen porter. Although I still couldn't hear them clearly I got the impression that the subject under discussion was football. Which surprised me a little – I hadn't been aware of Mukti's interest in sport of any kind.

Clouds of steam were rising in great big warm puffs from an assortment of gleaming cooking vessels arranged on the hob, obscuring the clergyman's face as he good-humouredly tilted backwards, rocking back and forth, nodding away there, on his heels. Whatever Mukti was saying to the porter it was clearly amusing. Perhaps he was telling him about his clever little plan – how he had taken over my case himself, and was making great progress, getting all the news about Marcus Otoyo. He doesn't even realise he's telling me, poor old McCool, he was probably saying. But I thought no more about it. I had had it up to here, thinking about Indians. The whole disgusting farce had been exposed and that was all I needed to know.

Mukti was all ears now, leaning forward, hanging on his visitor's every word. The puffs of steam dissipated, at long last providing me with a much clearer view. The clergyman had turned around, and I could see him now plainly in his charcoal-grey suit. Poor old Mukti – as I say, he had assumed it was some grudge I was harbouring towards Canon Burgess and perhaps the Catholic Church in general that had prompted me, conveniently providing my motivation. Which was utter nonsense, of course, as I have said. Visitors just didn't figure in the equation.

At long last they concluded their conversation and were preparing to say goodbye. Dr Mukti was waving as his visitor smiled and turned on his heel. Some chips were boiling in a tank, sunk deep in oil, with the handle of a wire basket protruding over the edge. It was convenient for me that the visitor's departure had been temporarily suspended, what with the psychiatrist somehow having caught his foot in the spars of a pallet as his companion patiently and bemusedly assisted him. They were much too preoccupied with this to notice anything when I finally emerged from my place of concealment and walked right up to them, swinging the wire basket in a wide arc – bringing it forward, even if I say so myself, in an extremely precise, almost perfectly judged movement. But, unfortunately, missing both Mukti and his companion completely with the result that one of the kitchen maids managed to skid on the discharged liquid, falling forward awkwardly, and somehow in the process managing to knock over a vat of boiling water, just as the so-called priest was trying to manoeuvre himself backwards. The scream that followed – it really was appalling.

The whole episode turned out to be a complete disaster. I heard later that the poor man had sustained horrendous burns. As they led me away, down the corridor to the White Room, who should I see, only Pandit passing by the window, breezing along in her Birkenstocks with her folder. As they turned the key and roughly pushed me inside.

Yes, the unfortunate 'boiling water' episode really did prove to be the most lamentable affair in almost every conceivable respect and I was still doing my best to erase all trace of its memory as I crouched there in the corner of the White Room, chewing my nail and hugging my knees, thinking: Why is my mind so soggy and dull? Then what happened – it started again. The noise, I mean. A kind of furtive scratching behind the grid. I braced myself, tentatively, for a reappearance. By the Indian Tom Thumb, I suppose you might call him.

In Wattles Lane in Cullymore long ago there lived a carpenter by the name of Half-inch Lynch, and it was him I was thinking of now as I found myself staring directly at the ventilation grid. The familiar sensation – that vaguely pleasurable tingling – had resumed as I felt my shoulders begin to elevate and already sensed the words as they formed on my lips. Well, well, I could hear myself saying, if it isn't Mukti the Indian giant! Only to find my arrogance disappearing – almost immediately draining away, and with it all trace of self-composure and defiance.

For what emerged through that serrated brick-sized oblong was not in fact Mukti – or anyone else.

But, bewilderingly, the injured visitor's unfortunate brother, the alcoholic – the man who, out of the goodness of his heart, he had travelled a long distance to come and see. I received quite a shock when I realised who it was – not because I recognised him straight away, having descried him from time to time meandering dazedly through the grounds – but because of his disarming, dishevelled appearance.

You could see he was a man who had genuinely been through the mill.

– To hell and back, as Mike Corcoran used to say.

As he stood there, pleadingly, in his shabby plaid dressing gown, his eyes said: Help me! with his lower lip quivering.

It was clear from his manner that it required a massive effort on his part even to think of speaking.

– You might think you know what you're doing, he said, raising an accusatory, tremulous finger, but you don't, Christopher. You don't know how good a man my brother is. He goes out of his way to come here every week. He listens so attentively, keeps returning, even when I disappoint him. And, God knows, many times have I done that. Only for him I'd never have known happiness. What comfort I ever knew is entirely because of him. In his efforts to protect me he has run the risk of his own life being ruined. His wife has pleaded with him to disown me altogether. But he never will. He says it's his duty to protect me from myself.

I covered my eyes and when I looked up he had gone, with the ventilation grid now seeming as dull and unremarkable and as ordinary as ever.

I'm fortunate enough to be able to say that I didn't let it get to me completely after that. For more than anything I had to stay strong, no matter how attractive at times it might appear just to collapse, capitulate entirely. To submit to the desire to call him back and tell him – to explain that more than anybody I *did* understand. Understand more than he'd ever know.

For I'd nearly gone under myself for the very same reasons: when the tide of emotion becomes literally a tsunami – takes over and becomes completely unmanageable. An all-engulfing wave that consumes, defeating sense, it seems, for ever.

Which was the reason I had found myself going up to Ethel Baird's. Nothing had been rational about that decision. I just couldn't stop thinking: Ethel will know. Ethel will understand. She'll explain all the mysteries to me. I had those lovely memories of her too, but I couldn't ascertain, not for certain, whether they were imagined or real.

Back in the Nook, when she knew Lady Thornton and Ethel were coming to visit, Dimpie would get so excited that she'd be dressing herself up for three or four days. To do her best to make herself 'respectable' for the Protestants, she said. Although, to be honest, what they must have made of the near-scarecrow that admitted them into the Nook can only be imagined. Wee Dimpie with her hairnets and her aprons and fishermen's sweaters and floppy old wellington boots, well, she was never going to be confused with Viscountess Rothermere or Dowager Fforbes-Maitland. But, being who they were, our visitors would never pass comment on such things. They would never draw attention to anything so vulgar. And the reason for that was – because they had access to the mystery of 'class'. There would always be tears in Dimpie's eyes as she waved 'the ladies' goodbye. She told me she loved them more than any Catholic.

– Catholics are liars, so they are, she would insist. Our ones is all twisters from birth. Let you down a bagful every time. Protestants bes odd – ignore you by times. But they'll always keep their word. Full of mysteries, they bes. You never know what goes on in their heads, they're up there so far and you can't get at them. Mysteries is what they be full of, Christy. But your mother, Lady Thornton. She's the best, the bestest quality of all.

All of those thoughts had been uppermost in my mind that day I'd had the disagreement with Marcus. As I wandered confusedly about the town, trying to make sense of what had just happened – doing my best to comprehend his hostile reaction. I was deeply cast down – to be honest, hopelessly perplexed. Which was why I went out to the greenhouse, of course – in the hope of seeing Evelyn Dooris. Who knew Otoyo better than anyone.

After that incident – I could still see his cold, disdainful expression – I would have given anything to be able to behave like Henry Thornton. To be capable of completely sublimating my feelings – my only hope of survival now. I couldn't, however – discovering, crushingly, that it was to prove quite beyond me. Once a Catholic, always a Catholic. Carberry's spiritually infirm genes were still in me.

I lacked the discipline, the reason and rigour.

You can't be hard if your nature is soft.

You can't be strong if your nature is weak.

Goodbye, Henry Thornton. I failed you, I'm afraid, I told myself. I'm one of them. I'm lower than the dog. Incapable of muscular detachment, alien to the concept of indifference, I am subordinated entirely by the forces of iniquitous, dissolute emotion. I haven't been chosen. I'm beyond the gates. Fated to remain outside the high windows for ever.

– It's a mystery, then, I heard Henry Thornton say triumphantly, and one to which you'll never find the key. And why you will always be vitiated, degenerate.

That was why I found myself, in a misty haze, making my

way up Ethel's driveway. Hoping against hope that she herself might open the door. That those high French windows at last would admit me and as she warmly opened them, I'd finally hear someone say:

– It's Christopher Thornton, our own Protestant kind!

11 In the Cathedral

And that is exactly what I wanted to feel as I sat there that day in Ethel Baird's neat and tidy suburban parlour – impossibly organised in that domestic, near-perfect Protestant way. But in point of fact was actually feeling quite desolate, still gripping *A Child's Garden of Verses* in my hand, asking Ethel would she mind playing the tune.

– Please will you play it, Ethel – 'Abide With Me'.

– What's wrong with you, Christopher? I can still remember her saying. You seem so pale, quite out of sorts. Do you want me, perhaps, to get you a drink of water?

I don't know why I did it, what it might have been that made me say it. I continued to be too emotional and did not exercise enough reason in the circumstances. That's the only defence I can make. My eagerness was excessive – I ought to have seen that it frightened the poor lady.

– Juh-juh-just play it, Ethel! Will you puh-please play the hymn! For kuh-kuh-Christ's sake!

I had no right whatever to address her in such a fashion. It was shameful, really, when I look back on it now. Ironically, I could feel Henry Thornton's presence so strongly as I stood there. His picture was in a gilded frame on the mantelpiece – an old sepia photo, I thought, from the forties. He was standing in the grounds of the Manor, attired, as always, formally, in his worsted tweed suit. Holding my mother's hand and looking out as if to say: He thinks that this will change things. He thinks coming up to Ethel's will do it. He's a fool, of course. The mystery is much much deeper than that. As of course it has to be. Otherwise riff-raff like that would routinely be admitted to spoil everything.

My mother was wearing a tweed costume too. Standing there, impassively, beside him, with a cluster of cherries on her lapel. I think that might have been what gave me the idea. The idea, I mean, of asking Ethel to put on the pillbox.

– The one, I mean, that you used to wear to Dimpie's. Do you still have it?

As it turned out, she did. And now, she might have been at any Sabbath service as she sat there on the piano stool wearing it, the milky notes of the plaintive melody lilting out into the evening, as Ethel sang and played, with pale trembling hands:

> *–Swift to its close ebbs out life's little day*
> *Earth's joys grow dim; its glories pass away*
> *Change and decay in all around I see;*
> *O Thou who changest not, abide with me.*

All I could see, as I sat there listening in that beeswax-heavy drawing room with its small china ornaments and pictures of soldiers from the First World War, was Henry Thornton – explaining, 'for the very last time', why he would never allow me to cross the threshold of the Manor.

– The only thing you're good at, and that much I will acknowledge, McCool, is being a bastard. You are quite excellent at that. And for that very reason, you will never gain entrance.

– Ethel Baird, I said, will you hold me?

– What? said Ethel, obsessively twisting the buttons on her lambswool cardigan. Her face was white.

– Puh-please, I implored her.

I could think of nothing else.

She continued agitatedly plying the buttons, tugging the hem of her tweed skirt down below her knees.

My voice was shaking as, exhausted, I took her hand and, as gently as I could, said:

– It's going to be OK, Ethel, it is really. This is the way it always should have been.

As, ever so gently, I climbed on to her lap. In a world of my own then as I held her hand and she turned the pages. And I gazed at the illustration over which the poem was printed, a boy with wide eyes sucking his thumb as he viewed the cosmos:

> – *The lights from the parlour and kitchen shone out*
> *Through the blinds and the windows and bars;*
> *And high overhead and all moving about,*
> *There were thousands of millions of stars.*
> *There ne'er were such thousands of leaves on a tree,*
> *Nor of people in church or the . . .*

– Oh Ethel, I said, as soothingly, reassuringly, my heavy eyelids began to fall, and I rested my head on her shoulder, bathed in the soothing glow of the fire. Thinking of Henry Thornton as he stood behind the French windows, indifferently staring out. Unmoved by my plea:

– Please let me in, Father.

Just sitting there with Ethel beneath the heaventree of stars, repeating the lines of the poem with her. Before all of a sudden, quite unexpectedly, she jerked, the book slipping from her grasp. And the next thing I knew she was lying on the floor.

What's perhaps most regrettable, even arguably unforgivable about the whole thing is that I left Ethel's without telephoning an ambulance. I ought to have – what had happened was that she'd sustained a coronary but all I kept thinking of was why I'd made a fool of myself with Marcus Otoyo. I've gone and made a fool of myself with him – there seemed to be nothing else in my mind. And I have no doubt whatsoever that that was what impelled me, whether I was aware of it or not, towards the cathedral in the first place. Of course it was childish – childish and stupid. For nothing could now possibly alter the way that things had happened. I was considered a fool by Marcus Otoyo. Not just a fool – worse than that.

Just as soon as I had pushed open the door of the cathedral I had seen the statue standing right in front of me – in the same place, before the high altar, where it had been specially positioned for the play, *The Soul's Ascent: Saints You May Not Know*. Yes, there he was, Blessed Martin de Porres, the dark-skinned Hispanic devotee of Christ. Who, as played by Marcus Otoyo, by unchallenged consensus, had been the unquestioned star of the show. As I stood there staring at the statue in the aisle, it exerted a powerful effect on me, the vivid memory – of Marcus as he read out the narrative:

– *And I John saw the holy city, new Jerusalem, coming down from God out of heaven, prepared as a bride adorned for her husband.*

His enunciation had been almost perfect. I recalled it vividly, exulting in its precision and passion. And it was then that I heard them: those resonant, poignant lyrics of 'The Holy City', the hymn that he had sung, and which had taken the breath of the congregation away. As I remained there, right in the middle of the centre aisle facing the altar, I found myself in an ancient marbled city, through whose streets I could see him proudly move as crusaders bent the knee outside its gates, and beheld in rapture that hilltop place, as beautiful to them as the vanished molten sunsets of childhood. Those gorgeous crimson piles of glory in the west, where clouds floated beyond the western heavens, from beyond whose pink magnificence now sounded the blast of martial trumpets. As, like a seraph's wing, in its flaming beauty, the singing voice of Marcus Otoyo now filled the cathedral, the abject devout proudly striking their breasts and, like the soldiers of old, weeping before the sight of that shining city:

> *– Last night I lay a-sleeping, there came a dream so fair,*
> *I stood in old Jerusalem beside the temple there.*
> *I heard the children singing and ever as they sang*
> *Methought the voice of angels –!*

– Shut up! I found myself involuntarily crying aloud, inexplicably waving my arms, and actually breaking into a run – before it dawned on me exactly what it was that I had just done.

The statue now lay in pieces before me, with splinters and scattered chunks reaching as far as the side altar. More than anything now I regret what I had written. The words crudely smeared in ash across the walls. Obscenities they had called them – rightly, for I accept now that that is what they were. There really can be no other description. Much of it remains vague even yet, although I can still remember the figure of an old lady retreating silently into the shadows. As I stood there, with the words I had written as blurred now before me as the rain upon the French windows of my imagination.

Fuck the holy city. Fuck all niggers.

They say that the sixties ended when the Rolling Stones played Altamont in '69. Well, for me that's not true. For me they climaxed in the cathedral that day. But the inevitable collapse had begun before that. Butlin's of Mosney – laughably, perhaps, that was our Altamont. That night when we went to the Beachcomber Bar. Or, more specifically, after I left it.

*   *   *

Up until that moment, things they had really been going so good. The sixties were really taking hold in Cullymore. There was colour everywhere, great ads, lots of fun, with a never-ending stream of people wandering in and out of Green Shield Stamps. And there were terrific bands playing in the Mayflower every weekend. As well as that, myself and Dolores were getting on like a house on fire. The Good Times bar was packed to the door. Which was terrific. It was great to have a place now where, like London or Paris or Milan, you could 'do your thing', yeah, 'get your kicks'. If, as they said, that happened to be 'your bag'.

The owner of the Good Times had done a great job – completely refurbishing the pub's interior. With the result that now there were not only posters of pop stars and singers – there was a giant one of the Beatles with their guru and one of Julie Christie swinging a Union Jack shopping bag – but also adverts for Smirnoff and cigarettes, with mountain streams flowing in super-saturated colours, the night skylines of famous cities glowing like something out of a fairy tale. Smart cocktails now were being served and a starry sky had been painted, twinkling away on the blue-domed ceiling. New chairs had been brought in that were shaped like artists' palettes and the fabulous chrome counter had – or so it was claimed – been imported from America. There was a cardboard effigy of John Fitzgerald Kennedy, with a glinting star leapfrogging off his pearly teeth.

Maybe it was inevitable that it would all end the way it did – after Dolores arrived on the scene. Who knows, had she not appeared I might never have bothered going down to Wattles Lane again, no matter how many invitations Marcus's mother extended. As a result, once more becoming prey to those old familiar confusing emotions whenever Marcus was in the vicinity. So consumed with *wounded pride and fallen hope and baffled desire*, as James Joyce had written in the book to which I had become so attached. C.J. McCool, only maybe not so cool, if you examined him closely. Anything but, in fact, truth to tell. C.J. Beatnik, C.J. Pops? Christopher Hot Jazz maybe more like, C.J. yes, extremely hot. Christopher anything but smooth and cool.

I knew it was only a matter of time: as gradually all pretence of becoming like Henry Thornton or any of his haughty empirical associates began to vanish and I surrendered so hopelessly but willingly to the feelings so eloquently described in *A Portrait*. Like the central character – if a fever quickened my pulse, or my heart began slowly to fold and fade with fear like a withering flower, I would pray intensely and the glories of Mary would hold my soul captive. My heart then, at last, would once more become calm. As I thought: Marcus is holy and so am I. Marcus is a Catholic and so am I. We two are Catholics, impelled by ardour to cast sin from our beings.

There were times when I would tremble, such was the singular enormity of the thought – that no one existed in the world, save us two: Marcus Otoyo and I, betrothed to Christ the King and his mother Mary.

As he stood there by the window of his kitchen, with his glossy curls shining, thinking to himself, or so it seemed: *I am the one who has been selected.* Though I despise the rough tribes of the cottages, their dull piety and the sickly smell of cheap hair oil with which they anoint their heads, it is I above all others who have been selected from amongst them and am now fated to join the order of Melchizedek, to bring glory to my parents and to the town of Cullymore. I am the unique, the uplifted – the elected. I alone am the tabernacle of Christ.

I could see him so clearly, pacing the floor of his room, head bent – hands clasped behind his back, deep in contemplation.

– Forget about Protestants and their hard, ungiving hearts, his expression seemed to suggest, forget about Henry Thornton, his well-bred abstinence and studied incuriosity. It is your surrender to tenderness which will be your salvation. Thus do I bless you, Christopher, my friend.

Sometimes I used to leave that cottage in a trance, scarcely hearing the words that Dolores addressed to me, as she took my arm and we negotiated the rainswept back lane, picking our way through the puddles and wet rubbish. Where Joyce's 'rough tribes' abided, and where once upon a time he too might have seen himself as a creature driven and derided by vanity. But where now, as we proceeded through the hoarse riot of those dwellings, nothing, for me, could have been further from the truth.

And for the first time in my life, I began to entertain the possibility of love. That night, for the first time writing, by the light of the moon, at my kitchen table:

For many days I had travelled, mindful above all that my journey at its end might prove to be fruitless and heartbreaking. And that when, at last, I gained the walls of the holiest city: the one that is called love and is sacred above all others. That no answer might be made to my knocking upon the gates of the new Jerusalem. That the echo of my plea might die as so often before, a hollow appeal destined to be heard by no human ear. Let me in, I might cry, above all things please let me in. Lift up these gates, for more than anything I need to belong. Only to find, as my soul was about to commit itself to despair, that the massive wooden gates swung effortlessly open and I was almost blinded as I stood there in a shaft of desert sun. Only for the sight to be returned to my eyes as I beheld him before me, Marcus Otoyo, attired in a fine tunic after the manner of a prince, with a crown of olives upon his head, as he extended his hand and in a soft voice told me:

– You are welcome, friend. To this holy place where we venerate and praise love. Come in. Now, Christopher Maximus, you are one for ever with us.

My soul was exalted as, at last, approaching dawn, I began my ascent of the stairs towards sleep.

12   Mr Wonderful

The night Man. United won the European Cup, the town erupted with a fervour greater than anything experienced ever before – with the streets and the squares sinking beneath a wavering sea of red banners and flags. Yet another effigy had appeared – this time of Sir Matt Busby, the successful team's manager, which had been erected outside the library.

At the counter of the Good Times they were gathered around Dolores like a pride of tomcats. As she, mischievously, patted her perm, batting her eyelashes and puckering her nose.

They asked her to sing another Peggy Lee.

– Sing 'I'm a Woman'! someone bawled.

It had gone down a storm in the bar the night before.

– Sing 'Black Coffee'!

– Let the dame sing whatever she likes.

Now she was provoking them towards all sorts of bravado. The word 'dame' was rarely heard in the town before. Not outside the pages of the *Mike Shayne* magazine. But around Dolly Mixtures, as she was now called, almost anything seemed to be possible. She might indeed have strolled out of that very publication, in semi-darkness lighting a cigarette with a tortoiseshell holder, circling crimson lips for men who went 'plumb crazy'.

Which was exactly what they did whenever she ascended the stage anew, to deliver a selection of sultry lounge ballads from what seemed to be an inexhaustible repertoire. Including Ruby Murray's much requested ditty, which she parodied for all it was worth, popping imaginary 'slices' into her mouth as she hoisted her skirts, wiggling coquettishly up and down the stage:

– *Yummy delisch! It's Miss O'Leary's Irish fruit cake!*

Standing in the spotlight in her black cocktail dress, kissing the air, proceeding to raise the sequined material to just a quarter-inch directly above her knee. Before suddenly abandoning Ruby Murray and her succulent confections and launching into her other much asked-for party piece, 'Dreamboat' by Alma Cogan:

– *Yew luvvable dreem – boat!*

When you heard Alma singing that bright and upbeat swinging melody it was like she was reaching out of the record to pinch everyone's cheeks individually. And that's what it was like now as the perky number jollied along:

– *You luvvable dreem – boat!*

After that, there was no shortage of men who declared their willingness to 'take on' Dolly Mixtures. To heartily administer a 'rub of the relic' to 'the Protestant'. Who, it was well known, were 'mad for it' in bed. Unlike Catholics, with whom you had to have a 'wrestling match', like Jackie Pallo or Billy Two Rivers. Thus it was extremely flattering and I would never dream of suggesting otherwise when it transpired that her affections, it appeared, were directed exclusively towards me. And to hear that she had privately confided in friends that she found me 'charming'.

– Chris McCool is my Mr Wonderful. My own special private Cullymore matinee idol. He's my Terence Stamp, my David Hemmings. He's Top of the Pops, he's Ready Steady Go.

As she crooned, clandestinely, to my absolute delight:

– *Why this trembling, Mr Wonderful . . . !*

Who would have ever dreamed it would end the way it did?

Such envy as we could excite in those days! The Happy Club, before its time. The Good Life Couple, *in town tonite!* at the Talk of the Town!

– He thinks he's all the pop star. He thinks he's Ringo Starr. Going around dressed in women's blouses and stripy slacks. What in God's name does Dolly see in him? Anyway, Carberry rode his auld mother, so he did, so he's a Fenian bastard, the very same as us.

Meaning, of course, of similar degraded and inferior status – whether my mother was a Protestant or not.

All of which was irrelevant to Dolores McCausland. Who now arrived regularly to visit me at the cottage.

– C.J. Pops, my own dandy boy, she'd say, slipping her warm hand underneath my shirt.

As the silver arm of the Bush hi-fi released Herman's Hermits on to the turntable.

And we'd snap our fingers and do the Watusi:

– No milk today, my love has gone away!

Except that she hadn't. She was right there in the thrillsville, doing the twist in a kitchen in Cullymore.

My problem, essentially – it wasn't really all that much of a mystery, when you got down to it – was one of excessive sensitivity and feeling. Unsustainable levels of emotion, pure and simple. And if Mukti had been doing his job – had asked me properly, for a start, instead of trying to pull fast ones – he'd have known that.

Stuh-stuh-stupid fucking Indian midget.

What's perhaps more regrettable than anything about the early days is that, in the beginning, it had been really terrific associating with Dolly. Without a doubt, she had been the most exciting thing to happen to me or the town for years. Thanks to that thickly lacquered blonde hair of hers and those long painted nails – not forgetting the exquisitely enticing, extremely shapely derrière. And the light chiffon scarves which she knotted around her neck, the manner in which she fingered her pearls as she spoke: in a husky, hypnotising Marlene Dietrich-style voice, the consequence of forty cigarettes a day. Sometimes, out of mischief, especially after a number of gins, she would cheekily say the most outrageous things, almost as if it were her entitlement as a Protestant, particularly where subjects of a 'bluish' nature were concerned. She told me privately that she wasn't really religious – and that the only reason she sang hymns at all was to 'watch the Catholics getting annoyed'.

– They take it so seriously! she said. So insecure!

– Giddy Dolly, she twinkled as she squeezed my hand.

Sure enough, every Sunday morning in Wattles Lane you would hear her, impishly teasing the Catholics going to Mass. Standing in the lane as though rehearsing for a concert – a private recital of favourite Protestant hymns: 'Open the Gates of the Temple', 'All People That on Earth Do Dwell' and, most notable of all, 'Abide With Me'.

But in the Nook late at night, it tended not to be hymns that we sang. No, the melodies Dolly crooned in the moonlight were different. As we drank whisky and she lay there beside me. Humming 'Mr Wonderful' – to me and no one else. If only it could have continued like that for always.

– *It's a strange and tender magic you do . . .*

As we lay there, smoking, and she blew a tendril of smoke into my face, crooning away – until the first cock crew. And there she was again, looking longingly into my eyes. Or should I say the eyes which belonged to no one else but:

– Mr Wonderful.

It really was a magic time: in essence, like the stuff of all the great romantic songs. If unfortunately, again like many of them, ending badly. With its considerable quota of heartbreak, misunderstanding and bitterness.

13   The New Philosophy

I was chewing my nail in the White Room one day –
thinking about Dolores, actually, as it happened –
when, completely out of nowhere, this mad thumping
starts – nearly putting the heart crossways in me, to tell
the truth.

I flung myself backwards.

– Go to hell, do you hear?

Receiving no reply, then screeching in falsetto:

– I'm serious, friend!

Before I remembered that I had been informed the day
before that I was actually scheduled to vacate my spookily
blanched accommodations. To be released under certain
conditions. I would be allowed out now – but only daily,
and not for more than an hour each time.

I had become so accustomed to my new home, I soon
realised, as we strode along the corridor towards the recre-
ation area, that I was afraid that I might actually be rendered
unhappy by ever having bothered to vacate it at all. When
who should I see, only Mike Corcoran standing grinning
there, waiting for me in the doorway. Puffing away with a
roll-up between his fingers.

– Put that fucking thing out! says the orderly. Don't you know you're not supposed to be smoking in here!

But kind of affectionately for it's always been hard to dislike old Mike Corcoran.

I had forgotten, in fact, just how fond I actually was of the man myself until the two of us happened to be sitting there watching the telly when he starts laughing. He's outrageous really, to be honest about it. I mean, all you can see is the Twin Towers falling in slow motion and all these poor unfortunate people leaping, literally plummeting there to their deaths, as Mike leans over and says:

– Boys, but I love Twizzlers. Maybe you'd like a Twizzler, Pops?

For a minute I don't have a clue what he's talking about – but then I see it in his hand, a little brown stem that he informs me is 'beef jerky'.

– Ah Twizzlers, he says, just the job.

So there we are the two of us munching away as his jaws rotate and he says:

– Mighty Twizzlers, I love them so much! with the poor New York victims still hurtling tragically to their deaths.

But he's still laughing, so much so that eventually it gets the better of me and I have to say stop it, Mike, it's inappropriate and he says:

– Auld cunts! Black bastards! Look at them all there smashed up like jelly!

And then what happens the two of us start arguing. Until the orderly appears, getting ready to fold the arms. Until he realises it's not all that serious. Well, serious, maybe – but not enough for us to come to blows.

All the same I had to acknowledge – even if I chose not to admit it – that there was a certain amount of sense in what Mike Corcoran had to say. After all, he insisted, if it can't be changed – if there's nothing at all you can do to alter the situation, what's the use in going around moping about it?

– You might as well laugh at the poor old jellymen, he says, and he stretches his legs, raising his eyebrow and saying:

– Twizzler, perhaps?

Big Brother was on for a while after that. But no surprises – it was the same old tiresome drivel trotted out: *Four-twenty-five in the Big Brother household.* Then some divorcee starts on about her 'feelings' and how the rest of the 'inmates' are abusing her and 'having a go'. Before bursting into tears as the rest of the tenants trail across the floor to swamp her in 'huggy love' – an unctuous and patently insincere embrace. The Balloon People have arrived, I thought, with all features erased as if by a massive celestial thumb. I looked at the screen – and all I could see were their host-heads staring back.

– The Orbs, I said, numinous, remote. For them engagement with the real world is no longer necessary. They live in TV in a world of white wax.

– The Eggmen, laughed Mike, they are the Eggmen, C.J., that's what they are. The fucking walnuts is what they are.

The humour had gone off me for telly, though. I was kind of looking forward to retiring, to tell the truth.

And all the way back to the White Room I could not keep from thinking that, simply by choosing a few simple words, Mike had created a whole new philosophy. With the result that, when I got back inside, the more I considered the substance of what he'd been saying, the more it began to seem like something of real worth. Definitely to be investigated further. Maybe I'd write a few notes about it, I thought. 'The New Philosophy, the Twizzlers Who Do Not Care'. I was in the middle of thinking up the first few opening sentences when – suddenly! – I found myself staring alarmingly at a corner of the room. Bracing myself for the first sound of activity in behind the ventilation grid.

Why, there wasn't even so much as a whisper, not a sound.

It was then that I started reflecting on the whole 'Tom Thumb' business with Mukti. And how stupid it all began to seem. I mean, a diminutive Indian doctor. What had I been thinking?

I was embarrassed beyond words, to tell you the truth.

But then I thought about Mike's new philosophy and it cheered me up no end. It was really the best laugh I'd had in quite a while. As Fat Curly the warm-up comedian in the Good Times always says:

– *Och come on, me auld muckers! Surely youse have to laugh!*

Except that, after a while, it didn't seem all that easy to do it, no matter how many amusing things you thought of, Twizzlers or anything. It was as if your smile seemed strained, as if you were trying too hard or something. It

seemed kind of forced, so tight that it hurt. So tight that it –
I don't know. So tight that it . . . it's hard to say . . . it's
difficult, you know? It's . . . duh-duh-difficult, that's all,
just duh-difficult . . . duh-duh-duh-diff . . .

14 A City Devastated

It wasn't long after the European Cup that a new record shop opened in the town – right next door to the Good Times bar.

And it was around then too that the first rumours began to surface about an impending visit to the town by the sensational chart-topper Clodagh Rodgers, whose number-one hit 'Come Back and Shake Me' was requested as often in the record shop now as anything by the Beatles. But all of this was as nothing to the opening of Colette's, the brand-new hair salon in the centre of the square, opposite the Green Shield shop. Already it was reported to be so popular that there were no appointments available until July. A noticeboard outside read: *The most modern salon in Europe.*

And it was into this already fabled emporium that Miss Dolly Mixtures, Dolores McCausland, one day confidently strolled, sporting her scarf in what she called the Babushka style, gaily knotted beneath her chin. Removing her Foster Grant sunglasses and breathing on to the lenses as she cooed – much to the chagrin of the nylon-caped incumbents, upon whom a small but palpably identifiable cloud of resentment now settled.

As they watched Dolly fold herself delicately into an easy chair, leafing through a copy of *Fashion Weekly*, into whose pages she gracefully vanished, as if she perceived herself somehow, quite effortlessly, to have taken possession of the town. Protestant entitlement, was how Henry Thornton might have described it. It's not as if I despise them, really, I recall him writing in one of his essays, for me they're more of an inconvenience, really, a mild irritation. Like naughty children, I suppose – or recalcitrant pets.

No one could say for definite where exactly the Clodagh Rodgers rumour had originated. Its authorship, however, was eventually attributed to none other than the record-shop owner himself, a well-known entrepreneur not long returned from England. Who had in fact left Cullymore in '58, never to be seen again apart from the occasional holiday in summer when he would arrive in off the boat, in his dark suit and thin tie looking like Ronnie Hilton, they said – a popular singer and bandleader of the fifties. He was a rich man now and had worked with all sorts of 'pop' bands in the UK, it was widely reported.

It has to be admitted that when Clodagh Rodgers didn't appear there was a great sense of being 'let down' in the town. But it didn't take long for that feeling to dissipate. For, as the name of the best pub in the area suggested, the late-sixties were indeed 'good times' and in any case Dave Glover and his band with the singer Muriel Day proved to be a more than adequate replacement.

In fact, among those present in the Mayflower Ballroom that night, were some who claimed to have seen Clodagh Rodgers perform in England and that she 'couldn't hold a candle' to Muriel Day.

– Who cares about Clodagh Rodgers anyway, someone said, she's probably a Protestant.

The fact that Muriel was one as well didn't seem to occur to or unduly bother anyone. She certainly looked it, with her beehive hair. No Catholic woman would have dared to sport such a coiffure at that time. For, if she did, she would be responsible, as Canon Burgess never tired of reminding his female congregation, 'for bringing a blush to the cheek of the Virgin Mary'.

It was around this time too that 'Fashion Show '69' was convened in the hotel and an emergency urban council meeting called to establish just exactly what it was that had 'gone on'. Quite a few members of the council hadn't been in favour of having the meeting at all for to tell the truth they were confused by the whole affair and privately confided that they couldn't 'for the life of them' understand how something like a fashion show could possibly come under the remit of the urban council.

But then this wasn't any old ordinary 'fashion show'.

It had been organised by Dolly Mixtures McCausland and the woman with whom she was staying at number 12 Wattles Lane. By the 'black fellow's' mother, as one of the members had indiscreetly phrased it.

– You know the young fellow, don't you? The lad they say has all the brains. Of course you do. The black lad.

It is no exaggeration to say that the fashion show caused a virtual sensation. For days before it had been the talk of the place.

Dolly Mixtures by now had acquired quite a reputation and not just in the Good Times public house. Everyone in Cullymore seemed now to know her. And her songs. Even the children sang about Miss O'Leary's cake, especially when they saw Dolly coming mincing through the puddles, delicately lifting her stiff lace petticoats, which were far more expensive-looking than anything seen before in Cullymore. Or, at least, that was how it appeared. Even though it might not have been true at all. For that was the thing about Protestants, somehow. Even if a Catholic had the same money as them – somehow the Protestant would always seem richer. As if Protestant money was worth more than Catholic. It was a kind of magic they appeared to possess. And Dolly Mixtures had it. It was as though a superior kind of light shone around her. Allowing her to do pretty much as she pleased. With no thought given to either consequence or restitution.

– *Mr Wonderful*, she would sing, twirling scarves and dancing around them, through the wet rubbish and broken eggshells of Wattles Lane.

– *Mr Wonderful, that's you!*

The children – though honoured – found themselves blushing and gasping in astonishment, as Dolly drew her baby-pink lambswool cardigan around her narrow shoulders and gave them a wave, puckering, before disappearing indoors.

Grown women took to following her down the main street, sneaking suddenly down back roads and entries for fear they might be spotted. It was as if they couldn't help themselves, as if they were being consumed by a virus of envy far more powerful and voracious than that to which they were accustomed. And it appeared to infect everyone, almost without exception. In this, the sixties, what exactly was happening to the town of Cullymore?

The Green Shield Stamp Centre had got properly into its stride by late August '68, and by the time the summer of '69 had come around, an even more extensive variety of house-hold appliances and fancy goods was being enthusiastically redeemed by the excited collectors and book-holders. Even the most modest of houses now were filling up with chintz armchairs and portable televisions, hairdryers, vacuum cleaners, garden furniture, toasters and expensive calf luggage that before you'd have only seen in advertisements. It was as if America and England had come to the town. First Blue Band Margarine, *Get Smart* and the Beatles, but more exciting even than any of them, the songbird Ruby Murray, in the form of Dolly Mixtures, who had the effect of making grown men turn into children. Turn into children and gibber like near-idiots.

As regards the 'Fashion Show '69' emergency meeting, there was one public representative in particular who had seemed over-zealous to the majority of councillors. And there was a reason for this. One day he had been in the supermarket buying cigarettes when he looked up to find himself standing beside a tall and curvaceous, slightly plump blonde woman who had her hair backcombed and lacquered, and who had dark upturned eyelashes and painted lips that seemed on the verge of taking off on their own.

Ever so daintily detaching themselves from her face. At least, that was what was going through the councillor's mind. As he stood there, trying to locate change in the folds of his trouser pockets, finding himself infuriated and affronted. What, he asked himself, is this all about? He hadn't come into the supermarket to be confronted by unnecessarily provocative sights such as this, he told himself.

But that was nothing to what was coming. Only seconds later, as a matter of fact, when, quite unexpectedly, he found himself staring in open-mouthed astonishment as, curling her lip, she gazed directly at him, giving her figure-hugging black dress the most provocative little *tug*.

Before patting her hips and for no reason exclaiming:
– *Oops!*

The councillor rolled out into the deafening clamour of the Cullymore afternoon. With confluent trickles of perspiration shining on his forehead. He stood in the edgy sanctuary of a dark alleyway, repeatedly clenching and unclenching his fists. It was this same official who had made the impassioned speech. Who had posed the definitive question to his colleagues: *What on earth was going on in Cullymore?*

103

At the fashion show Dolly had been wearing a beautifully cut A-line dress with matching black stilettos. Her unblemished appearance, as the MC had pointed out, was accentuated by her sparing use of Max Factor pancake make-up, whose brand was also responsible for her pastel pearly pink lip colour called Strawberry Meringue. Her gloves, it emerged, were by Dent's, and were a cream pair in cotton, always the hallmark of the lady.

The other ladies acquitted themselves admirably throughout the remainder of the show, it has to be said. But afterwards they too began to flock around Dolly, with even greater enthusiasm now than the men. Breathlessly plying her with questions about handbags – and whether she used a lip brush or not. It was as if the spotlight never seemed to desert her. The real Ruby Murray would have had her work cut out to compete – Ruby Murray, who could do no wrong in the UK charts.

– *Softly softly*, the women sighed as Dolly walked by, making heroic efforts not to savagely consume their pendulous, defeated underlips.

But more action was to follow later on in the Good Times.

Dolly had been sitting at the bar with some friends when Ronnie Hilton the owner called on her for a song. There was to be no dissent on this occasion either. That evening was declared 'the best so far!'. For no sooner had she ascended the stage than, without any warning whatsoever, she smacked her thigh and launched into a fast and furious up-tempo version of the Muriel Day hit 'Wages of Love', sassily curling the microphone cable, puckering her nose and pouting her lips as she did the twist right down to her hunkers.

The pub was completely packed now, going wild as Dolly Mixtures gave no indication of desisting, wiggling her ample hips and thrusting out her sequined bosom, snapping her fingers as she launched into 'Fruit Cake', raising her dress high as before. Wolf whistles soared and the fever intensified.

– *Yummy delisch!* sang Dolly, running her tongue along her lips as she sensuously swayed:

– *It's Miss O'Leary's Irish fruit cake!*

Her performance being so powerful that there wasn't a man present in the bar who didn't go home, thinking: I'm fantastic! For it's plainly obvious that Dolly finds it hard to physically resist – *me*!

Except that they were deceiving themselves, for the final number she sang that night – it was dedicated solely, well, to what person do you think?

Yes, the one and only, specially chosen *Mr Wonderful!*

So was it any wonder that the nascent Simon Templar, self-styled cool globetrotting bachelor of the sixties, would remain casually at the bar, sipping dry Martinis? For he was clearly moving into the big league now. As the diminuendo of the piano's tinkling treble gave way to Tony Bennett's secular hymn to the manifold delights of 'The Good Life'.

– You look beautiful, Miss McCausland, I said with a laugh, whenever, at last, she came waltzing over to join me.

Speaking in a kind of jet-set, transatlantic accent, which amused her. I was acting like I was Tony Bennett myself!

And she was even calling me 'baby' now – in that lovely cutesy sixties way. Giggling at things that weren't even so funny.

It was great. No, it was maj!

– Yeah, baby, it's a magic time!

– It's maj! Yeah, babes, it's maj!

It was the following Sunday that Canon Burgess delivered his sermon on the subject of nightdresses and their potential evils. It had been problematic, presumably, for him to make it – with a clergyman hardly likely to have been particularly well-informed about such a subject. Which had only been broached at all on account of the Dreamland lingerie brand: a selection of which had just gone on display in the window of the Green Shield Stamp showroom. For two books of stamps, the sign read, any 'go-ahead lady' in Cullymore who so wished could find herself the proud owner of the fabulous Dreamland nightie – a two-tier shortie with tiny lace cap-sleeves and frilled flounce.

The clergyman insisted to his congregation that he had privately been promised that the offending items would be removed without delay from the front of the window. This was what he had been discreetly assured. But, much to his regret, this, sadly, had not happened. Indeed, and much to the astonishment of the citizens of Cullymore, in the aftermath of the homily, exactly the opposite proved to be the case.

The original sign had been removed all right. Yes, it, without doubt, had been taken away. But now in its place, in italicised letters of the gaudiest frosted pink, was the announcement that Dreamland Foundations, in association with Green Shield Stamps, had agreed to sponsor the Cullymore Summer Lingerie Extravaganza, to be held in the Cullymore Arms Hotel that very week.

In the wake of this alarming development, yet another meeting was called in the urban council chambers and this time the aforementioned irate member had stormed out in a blind rage. It was the first time anyone could recall this actually happening. Certainly since any elected representative had been heard to utter the expletive 'fuck' in the chambers.

But on this occasion there was no enthusiasm for conflict – even debate. Perhaps the word 'lingerie' was perceived as being too essentially intimate in nature, encroaching too impudently on to the esoteric, vaporous privacy of what they perceived to be the world of women, breaching the boundaries of their sacred holiness. And so, at the risk of giving the unfortunate councillor a stroke – the subject was subtly but quite firmly dropped.

There were all sorts of rumours, predictably, circulating about Dolly. That she was definitely a Protestant everyone knew. There were intimations of her having been 'separated' from her husband in England, and that she had come to Cullymore to stay with her equally husbandless friend, Marcus Otoyo's mother. But no one individual was sufficiently informed to vouch for the veracity of any of this.

The suspicion then surfaced that she might be divorced. Which would have been unheard of in Cullymore at that time.

This came to represent another mystery – something that *they* did, meaning the Protestants and the English, with impunity. Like reading the *News of the World* paper. Which, not insignificantly, was perused weekly by Dolly, from cover to cover. Just as soon as she had finished singing her hymns in the lane. Yes, there she would sit turning its dubious pages, its shadowy photos depicting the exploits of 'runaway wives', not to mention various goings-on 'in the suburbs'. And government officials indicted for 'gross misconduct'.

– What's gross misconduct? Marcus had, shamefacedly, enquired of her one particular Sabbath morning, I was informed.

Which had amused her no end, she said.

– He really is the most innocent youth: destined for the priesthood. Such a loss, I sometimes think: he's so sweet and innocent – handsome, you know?

I made no reply – just kind of shrugged.

– You know, sometimes I catch him looking at me, she said, at my legs especially. How it makes me laugh!

I dismissed it. It meant nothing – why should it?

What was unusual about that? I asked myself. It did not surprise me greatly at all that Marcus Otoyo, being an essentially spiritual boy, which we all knew he was, might harbour, even awkwardly declare, certain affections for Dolores McCausland.

– He's so thoughtful, it's flattering, she would say,

twirling a loose strand of her fine blonde hair – in a kind of daze, as I recall.

But if it meant anything to me – if it bothered me in any way, then I did not show it. Indeed I encouraged her to indulge his innocent, adolescent excitements. As I lay there beside her looking into her eyes.

– *Such vehement passions!* I would think, recalling *A Portrait*.

As I thought of us there by the swaying green ocean – Marcus and I.

Being holy, he liked all kinds of hymns, she said. I hadn't asked her, she had brought up the subject completely out of nowhere. But being a Catholic boy at heart, she continued, there would always be a special place in his heart for hymns that tended to be of a more vivid and evocative cast. Tunes that evoked the colour of crimson, released in one's soul certain primitive emotions.

The songs of that kind for which he retained a special affection, she claimed, included 'Soul of My Saviour', 'To Jesus' Heart All Burning' and, of course, 'Faith of Our Fathers', with its stirring lines concerning blood and martyrology. Wherein a tender youth found himself done to death at the point of a sword.

– *His last end*, Marcus would sigh, almost lovingly, she told me.

– He writes too, you know. About the most wonderful things. Once he composed a little story about himself. He often does that. He's made up a character. He calls himself Marcus Minor in them. And me, his Ariadne.

– Does he now, I said, through thinning, defensive lips.

He had told her many such stories, she further elaborated a number of weeks later. I was confused by my feelings, finding myself hot and bothered as she continued. He would see certain people, she explained, standing numbed by his graveside: Dolores McCausland among them, clad in a black mantilla, erupting into fits of sobbing as she declared how his love for her had enabled her to see the light, to embrace what she called the 'Catholic mystery' – and become converted, to the amazement of all – to the code of Catholicism. Which she once would have regarded as uncivilised, indeed heathen.

– He loved me so much he gave his life, she would say. For me, Dolly Mixtures, he gave himself up and died.

After a while I began to laugh whenever she would tell me such stories. Which essentially were innocent, I succeeded in persuading myself, and had little or nothing to do with me. But still I shivered when I'd think of him as Marcus Minor, girdled in a loincloth, watching him slump lifelessly from a cold marble pillar, mourned by Dolly, tear-stained and helpless. But ultimately triumphant in the security of their love.

He told her once he dreamed he had died with her name upon his lips. They had been listening to *Hospitals' Requests* at the time, she said.

– You were holding my hand as I expired, he had told her.

And had actually taken her hand as he spoke, she laughed.

– The Church's gain is some unfortunate woman's loss, she joked. I could see that boy as a heartbreaker, believe me. I joke with him, you know, about his being Stevie Wonder.

Stevie Wonder was a young black prodigy, a popular vocalist at the time, and whose song 'My Cherie Amour' was the hit of the summer.

– I even let him try on my sunglasses. Stevie Wonder! I say and we laugh. Oh how we laugh!

They never missed the agony aunt programme *A Woman's World* on Saturdays, she told me.

– *Dear Frankie*, she had chuckled.

– *Dear Frankie, my boyfriend is a very puritanical man and basically does not like attractive women. He disapproves of make-up, sheer tights, jewellery, tight sweaters and jeans. He's had a number of girlfriends before me, but he gave them up because he said they were too pretty and flamboyant.*

– Would you give me up because I was too pretty and flamboyant, Marcus Minor? she had asked him.

– Never, my Ariadne, he had pledged, to the death I would defend you: and the holy love that we share together. Here in this private, radiant place. The holy city – the chambers of the heart.

Stroking my cheek as she lay there beside me.

– He takes it so seriously. He really is the most extraordinary boy. Such a dreamboat for some lucky girl!

How I hated her using that word. As I listened – my heart scourged with jealousy – I could see them crouched over the wooden cabinet: bathed in the electricity of the female mysteries that were being transmitted over the airwaves.

Most especially, of course, Protestant women, as Dolly Mixtures sighed by his side, her stiff glistening hair like some mythical, unbreachable tower. As she gazed down the valley to where he stood in his tunic in the midday haze, before the wooden gates and the ramparts of the city walls. Calling:

– *And I John saw the holy city!*

Marcus Minor Otoyo, courageous envoy, bracing himself to defend her honour.

– 'Love's City', he called that story, she told me, when, quite unexpectedly, I had snapped:

– *Oh for Christ's sake, Dolores, forget it!*

Which had prompted her to reply:

– Why, baby is upset! I do believe my Christopher is jealous! Come on, hon, it's just a bit of maj!

We made a laugh of it after that and right up until the time – some weeks later – when I discovered the envelope in her handbag, the whole thing had become more or less forgotten.

But I'd still smart whenever I thought of it, as she attended to her hair in the compact mirror.

– Imagine that, Christopher. And in one so young!

How foolish I had been. And all that one can say is – if there was innocence abroad in that irresponsible age that was the sixties, then it was I, Christopher McCool, one's hedonistic affectations notwithstanding, who best represented its embodiment.

Even to this day it still rings in my ears, the mocking muffled laughter I had heard that night. As they stood there together in the moonlit serenity of the holiday-camp chalet. That shocking night in Butlin's, after I had quit the Beachcomber Bar. To my horror, for even yet I can find no other word for it, finding myself witnessing, through the window of that modest, wind-whipped cabin, Dolores McCausland ever so confidently and proprietorially taking Marcus Otoyo by the hand, as she pressed it to her cheek, laughing now in that beguiling, crushing way. As she crooned a soft melody, gazing into his eyes as she continued with it:

– *My Cherie Amour, distant as the Milky Way!*

Desultorily, but with a steely inner conviction, lightly kissing each of his fingers. Singly, with great attention – before leading him patiently towards the small bed.

Leaving behind her a city in ruins.

113

15   My Friends the Stars

A city now which is almost as ancient as the old Cullymore, as we approach the end of the first decade of the twenty-first century. I have to say, though, that it's wonderful to have returned here after all this time, to have come back once more to the place of one's birth, one's own hometown, where, effectively, one was formed. Not that you'd recognise it – not in a million years. At least not at first. For, considering the speed of the changes that have taken place over the past two decades, it makes that of the sixties seem little more than a sluggish crawl.

It really all began with the advent of the prosperous nineties. Why, it might even be said that it's inaccurate to describe the place as a *town* any more, for what it is, more than anything now, is a satellite suburb of the city of Dublin. With people who, in my time, years ago, would have gone and had themselves a brain haemorrhage if you had dared to suggest that they travel more than twenty miles beyond their home to work now thinking nothing of a four-hour round trip daily. To toil in the many new basilicas of the future, the numerous financial hubs, call centres and silicon-chip compounds which have sprung up in the last decade or so – the brash fortresses of the prosperous new century.

Yes, 'the good times' of old, they seem so remote – so down at heel and dowdy as to be almost downright embarrassing for many people – now about as welcome as my daddy, Stan Carberry, turning up drunk at a Thornton society wedding. I have to say, though, in all honesty, with some small measure of wisdom at my disposal, the sagacity of age, call it what you will – that I largely tend to concur with this view. Even the Beatles seem to me somehow manufactured, their public image laughably contrived. With those incorrigibly gormless beaming smiles and semi-idiotic playground antics.

No, if you want 'the good times', there is no better period in which to be alive. Nobody will bother you – you can more or less do whatever you like. Because the great thing is that – no one will *care*. You can rest assured there will be no intervention. It makes the assertions of sixties freedom look so childish. Why, you don't even have to leave your room. It's all right there before you on your computer screen, a virtual highway replete with infinite, intoxicating possibilities. Even for someone of my advanced years. Of course there are the usual complaints, most notably by members of my own generation. The – ha ha! – trendsetters of yesteryear.

Since moving to the Cottages I have heard nothing from them but a succession of dreary whines. Yes, since time immemorial, you can always rely on the over-sixty-fives. If you paid any serious attention to them, you'd probably be too afraid ever to bother even getting out of bed. For fear of being murdered or stabbed – by the hordes of drug addicts and ex-mental-hospital crazies who purportedly roam the streets of our towns and cities.

All of it, as always, paranoid nonsense, of course.

By my reckoning, in fact, in my experience, I would have to say that never in its history has Ireland been a safer place. Or, for that matter, more contented with its lot. It's just age, I guess, as it always tends to be, and I daresay that, if I hadn't been so lucky in my life, I would probably have ended up the very same way.

If I hadn't been more fortunate than the great majority of the residents in these apartment buildings. The Cottages, as the complex is called, is a gated community of flats located near Barnageera village – not far from the Co. Dublin town of Rush, where St Catherine's Hospital is, in fact, situated – and which contains, unknown to the majority of the residents, a number of people similar to myself. Former patients of the hospital, that is, who, in the very same way as I, have been cured – but are still monitored, from time to time.

Although, to be honest, I am not aware of being watched or spied upon. There have been no prying eyes that I have identified, and I'm as happy and contented here as I think I really could possibly be. And for that, thanks I think, mainly, are due to another old friend from my hospital years – Mossie Phelan, great old trouper that he is. But who has been through his own share of trouble too, believe me. His own quota of social ostracism. He was accused of being a paedophile, you see – vilified and slandered to a quite appalling degree, really. And yes, it's him I have to thank for

116

my recent good fortune. For it was he, my old friend Mossie, who eventually made the scales disappear. Made them consummately fall from my eyes. To the point of embarrassment, actually, to be honest.

Which is ironic when you think that for that whole first year after he came to St Catherine's I had stubbornly refused to engage with the man, even to acknowledge his presence on the corridor. *Disgusting paedo*, I used to think, in exactly the same way as everyone else. Hanging's too good etc. etc. It was only when I got to know him and he began to tell me all about his experiences as a Catholic priest that I began to sit up and pay serious attention to the unfortunate man. With it soon becoming very plain indeed that Mossie Phelan was most certainly not a disgusting paedo and a damaged human being worthy of hanging but was extremely sincere and genuine in what he was saying.

And not only that – but also knew what he was talking about. And as far as he was concerned, I remember him telling me, it was not untrammelled hedonism or self-ishness that was at the heart of the malaise of the modern world.

– No, he said, it's not that at all. It's religion, Christopher.

He went on then to describe himself as a born-again fundamentalist. But a fundamentalist atheist, not a Christian. Subsequently plying me with various tomes on the subject. Notably *The God Delusion* by one Richard Dawkins.

The great thing about it all, though, was that Mossie wasn't pushy. The way that he saw it – you could take them or leave them, his views on the subject. But he left you in no doubt as to his distaste for Christian dogma – that of Catholicism in particular. He was invigorated, he told me, by the Church's recent troubles, and derived great satisfaction from watching it teetering along helplessly as it went, pawing its way through this fast-altering epoch like some burlesque, bleary-eyed drunk.

– Collapsing, now a pathetic superannuated colossus, as we enter the new world.

It was this man and he alone who facilitated my entry into this 'new time', enabled me to find a place in this bewilderingly changing world, side by side with my fellow human beings. Indeed who knows, without the assistance of Mossie Phelan, I might never have been in a position to vacate that old White Room, and find myself here in this fine apartment of bliss rediscovered. Lying here beside the charming Vesna Krapotnik every night, enjoying our own 'good times' here in our very own little club, our lounge – womb of ecstasy, where I peruse my treasury nightly, and together we recite Stevenson's 'Escape at Bedtime'. Ably assisted in our continued pursuit of ecstasy by the voice of Tony Bennett, a tasty daiquiri and, as always, a little puff on a Peter Stuyvesant (*the international passport to smoking pleasure*). Not forgetting, of course, my old friends the stars. Who, reliable as ever, twinkle beyond the blue-domed ceiling. As the pages of *A Child's*

Garden of Verses rise and slowly fall and I gaze into the eyes of my dearly beloved Vesna.

I will always remain eternally grateful to Mossie Phelan for all of his moral support in the past. For showing me things and never harbouring resentment for my offhand treatment of him in the beginning. Quite simply, without him, I don't think I would ever have survived. Most certainly, would never have reached the place where I am now – having a wife like Vesna and a love-nest quite as sumptuous as this.

I mean, who, back then, would ever have dreamed of owning not one but two state-of-the-art Bravia flatscreen plasmas. Not to mention the state-of-the-art paper-thin Macintosh computer that the authorities have generously donated to me. Which provide me with endless hours of compelling entertainment.

The young instructor – complete with tufty sixties beatnik beard – was even good enough to spend a long time giving me a Mac demonstration. So now I literally spend hours on the machine. For my generation, I would be inclined to suggest, I think it has taken the place of the old-time steam radio. Gone now are *Dear Frankie, Hospitals' Requests, Down the Country* and *Intermediate Girls' Hockey*, and in their place *Big Brother* and *Oprah* and *Celebrity Love Island* and *Makeover Special. Happy Househunters in the Sun* is a particular favourite of mine. As well, of course, as the many new websites one tends to discover almost daily. *Perfidia.com* is the one I continue to access on a regular basis, communicating with others who happen to be online for the same reason as myself. People who've been hurt in a similar way, who've been on the receiving end of treachery in love, with people they have formerly adored – the very same as I had Vesna.

It used to pleasure me greatly, back in St Catherine's, joining with Mossie in denouncing Catholicism. I think it was only after meeting him *(Fucking God! Fucking Martin de Porres! Fucking love! Fucking Jerusalem!)* that I began to realise I was approaching a time when my emotional troubles would at last be behind me. In other words that, at last, I would be cured. Not only that but completely so.

Just as, later on, I came to see vividly that the very same conclusion could now be applied to the feelings I'd once harboured for a certain young fellow called Marcus Otoyo. It had been stupid of me, I now realised, ever to have dwelt for so long on the so-called 'otherness' of his personality. To have ascribed all sorts of exceptional qualities to Marcus's nature, purportedly intense spiritual feelings which had existed nowhere except within the confines of my own suggestible imagination. What I came, more than anything, to conclude was that, in fact, what had been taking place with that seventeen-year-old boy was that I had been projecting my own needs and desires on to him. And was using both him and the textures and colours and beliefs of Catholicism to try and find a place, I suppose, a home for my own particular 'excitable passions'.

For which, up until that point, I had found no parallel apart from the pages of James Joyce's novel. And which now, when I think of, tends only to make me laugh. So adolescent does it seem, I mean. Especially when you consider that its author – who was the last word in vehemence – had eventually renounced that very faith, with some theatricality quite publicly disdaining it, after all his talk of 'absolution', 'restitution', of 'tremblings' etc., of 'myrtle' and 'lavender'.

Not to mention the ubiquitous 'swooning souls'!

What's great about age is that you at last see things clearly. You review your life and what you see is the comedy. As you flush at the things you believed when you were young. When so replete are you with possibility that you'll tend to believe in almost anything that's available, and the more romantically impossible the better.

Appraising it now, in retrospect, it seems clear that the only reason Marcus Otoyo had been reading *A Portrait*, in fact, had had it in his possession at all, was because he had no choice – it being a prescribed text on his examination course at school.

After a few little chats in the hospital, it didn't take Mossie long to spot the problem.

– You're certainly more a natural Catholic than you would be a Protestant, Christopher, I would have to say, he told me, for a Protestant would have planned the whole thing rationally – as they always do, as it is in their make-up to do. You, on the other hand, capitulated almost entirely to your emotions. To longings, in fact, plainly evident in your unrealistic, would-be Joycean elevation of a mildly interesting and reasonably intelligent but otherwise unremarkable adolescent. He was just an ordinary growing boy, C.J. You mythologised him: imagined him out of all existence, that's all. You're a hopeless romantic, to a ludicrous degree. There was nothing special about Marcus Otoyo, as you subsequently discovered. He was merely a diligent scholar with an admittedly fine singing voice but a very ordinary intelligence, even if he did display a certain facility with words in his letters and other writings. But you over-valued that too, I think, Christopher. Yes, you did. It too was no more remarkable than a lot of the musings of the average spiritually inclined youth. Disappointing, perhaps, but those are the facts. Which, of course, you understand now.

What a wonderful man Mossie Phelan was – and to think of how his intuition and cleverness had been wasted for so long on so much superstitious Catholic mumbo-jumbo, really: ascensions, miracles, transubstantiations, the mystical body, the communion of saints and all the rest of it.

It's hilarious, really it is. Hilarious, for sure, if it wasn't so – well, so damned embarrassing, really.

But it's all over now, and in the end that's, as always, all that matters.

I think if you were to ask me what the thing I most admire about modern life as it's lived in this the early part of the twenty-first century is it is the single simple fact that no one now would dare impinge on another's privacy. No one claims the right to interfere. Not like the old days when one's life seemed to be lived under the shadow of omni-present detectives, Pinkertons indeed – effectively one's neighbours. Of every hue and colour, from old ladies in housecoats to fat men in darkened bars. Everyone was watching, cupping hands and delivering judgements. Now that's ended. They don't care enough. About your business, the details of your private affairs. Indeed, I would go so far as to say that no one cares about anything any more. Gossip has died and a strange peaceful silence over-hangs the Plaza, with the only interruption being the static of the rotating plasmas, but which no one is aware of as their presence is constant. While, under the awning, the host-heads continue to abide, *en famille*, passing wine across the table. It's like a clean breath has passed invisibly across the world. Effortlessly, it seems, ending generations of small-town tittle-tattle, and with it all the concomitant hypocrisy.

I mean, in total, there are thirteen other residents in this block and I'm not on speaking terms with any of them. In white-wax apartments orb-heads pass on the stairs. Such peace in anonymity never before known in Ireland. Even a scream has lost its power. To disturb the still, chill peace of our apartment building. Why, only just the other day, I feel certain, if I had been so unlucky as to meet any of the neighbours in the elevator whilst accompanied by the sullen brat of a youth I had encountered by chance in the Plaza – to amuse myself, I had christened him Stevie Wonder – I am pretty convinced there would have been scarcely any protest, little or no form of repercussion. The Eggmen, as Mike calls them, would have regarded me, recorded what was taking place. Before, delicately, with a foggy kind of lyricism, floating onward up the stairs, their privacy once more sealed with a delicate, mannerly but non-negotiable click.

For who concerns themselves with such inconveniences now? With such unnecessary and time-consuming diversions? It's behaviour which belongs to a prelapsarian age.

When self-appointed custodians of morality took it upon themselves to administer merciless beatings, to encroach upon humble cottages called the Nook under cover of darkness, before delivering summary judgements with the tacit approval of a cowed community, with the result that one was packed off, undefended, to a sterile, remorseless institution, hopefully to be forgotten for ever. By order of the state and her ally Mother Church, signed Canon Burgess and all his associates from Bernie's Bar in Cullymore.

No, I welcome the fact that those times are consigned to history. For these cleaner, more clinical, perhaps, but distinctly pronouncing aggressively individual times (Margaret Thatcher, perhaps, began it, with her statement regarding society, effectively pronouncing that there is no such thing) tend to offer much more, and to an infinitely greater number of people, than anything which would have been accessible in the past, making the grandiose claims of the consumer era, the great permissive age of opportunity, 'the sixties', appear laughable. With that undertow of fierce conservatism which was still in existence throughout that whole period, lurking and ever ready to bare its face, remove its mask. Why, even to recall that awful night, in particular those few moments just before the Inquisition from Bernie's descended on the Nook

– is to facilitate the return of the most dreadful feelings. And alter one's countenance so that it mimics that drawn, ascetic aspect of old. When one's approach of the looking glass revealed something almost unearthly – a soul on the verge of utter catastrophe.

A process which had, in fact, begun in earnest in the late summer of 1969. Its most significant episode, perhaps, being represented by the discovery I'd made – the letter which, to my horror, I had found in Dolly's handbag. But the seeds of which – regrettably, I have to say – had been sown much earlier.

I ought never to have accepted the invitation to go on the vacation, to accompany them both on 'a little holiday'. It ought never to have been permitted in the first place. It was wholly irresponsible of his mother to allow it, but of course that's easy to say – Dolores McCausland could be very persuasive. It had been stipulated that we were all to reside in our separate accommodations. But how credulous could his poor deluded mother have been? Did she think that Marcus was so supremely holy and devout that he would continue, inevitably, to remain beyond the bounds of temptation? Just how innocent can you be?

This much is clear: I ought never to have gone near that holiday camp. I ought to have advanced a plausible excuse. I ought to have firmly said no, in actual fact.

No!

No, Dolly, I'm afraid I can't go.

It's unfortunate but that's all there is to it.

That I couldn't bring myself to do something as un-complicated and simple as that. But that is the case. Once I heard that *he'd* be going.

I had even packed *A Portrait*. With this idea in my head that somehow we'd find an opportunity to read it together. My eyes still burn with anguish and resentment. When I think of her lying there beside me in the Nook, expressing her affection for me, whispering 'Mr Wonderful', just before the cockerel crowed in the dawn:

– You're not really going to stay here, are you, Christopher? Spend the rest of your days here, working on this silly old farm, a man of your abilities and intelligence? What's to stop us going to London? What fun we'd have: we might even see the Beatles. I could ask them to play my favourite song.

– What's that? I remember asking.

– 'Mr Wonderful', she said, as she twinkled a little and gave a little shiver, before throwing her arm around my waist, her chest rising and falling as she gradually fell asleep.

Try as I might, for the remainder of the entire night I couldn't close my eyes. All I could think of, in spite of myself, were the words: *It was his own soul going forth to experience, unfolding itself sin by sin, spreading abroad the bale-fire of its burning stars and folding back upon itself, fading slowly.*

16 Vesna Krapotnik, Catholic

Every morning now when I wake up in the Happy Club, I find myself succumbing to sensations of sheer delight and amazement: when I reflect on just how fortunate I am – finding myself alive at all. Much less the sharing tenant of a freshly decorated, state-of-the-art apartment, with its chess table, as I say, its silk Moroccan cushions and Peter Blake prints. Not to mention the expensive carpeting and fittings throughout, filled with light that streams through the wide picture window that at night admits, once more, my friends the stars – the blue fruit of heaven.

But, no matter how well your life is going, no matter how smooth everything seems to be, certain things, somehow, will always continue to irritate. Like that pesky imp, that infuriating little black bastard I mentioned earlier, whom I happened to meet, quite by chance, one day on the Plaza. Of course, in spite of his fulsome assurances to the contrary, when I eventually brought him back to the apartment it transpired that the liar could scarcely read at all. Never mind understand the first thing I'd been talking about. I slammed the book down on the table again. *Portrait*. With the portrait of Joyce louchely reclining on a chaise longue.

– Will you just fucking read it, Stevie Wonder! I bawled at him. Just read it and then go!

It was the Penguin edition. Not that it mattered what edition it was, as very soon I became aware that I was completely and utterly wasting my time. He was useless – worse than useless. Such an uncultured, duplicitous little good-for-nothing.

– Oh yes, mister, yes, I can read it, of course I can, it will only cost you fifty euro.

But his lies weren't the reason I struck him with my meerschaum cane. And quite forcibly too, to the extent that his stupid black blood stained it.

No, he had started implying this physical thing again. Making, at first hesitant, unwholesome imputations.

– You impertinent little wretch! I said, raising my stick. Oh you manipulative little twister, I said – with a succession of blows forcibly raining down. I have to admit – I really was furious.

– What a fool I was to have expected either competence or civility. Get out, Wonder! Go on – clear off, and don't come back!

I tugged him by the collar, dispatching him forthwith into the deserted corridor. Flinging a handful of coins in his wake, I called after him:

– Be damned to you, ingrate!

As I sat at the table with my head in my hands, turning the fragile brown pages of the book.

Feeling sick and dejected, to tell you the truth.

* * *

128

Which is why, that very night, I approached Vesna and told her again that I loved her, that I felt I meant it more than ever. Kissing the back of her hand as we listened to Tony Bennett, talking about the old times and how far we had come, after all this time. She said she was glad she didn't lie to me any more. Because of course, regrettable though it might be, she had always had that tendency. She had even done it on our very first meeting. Had looked me in the face and lied through her teeth, to be honest. As we sat beneath the awning outside the café in the Plaza. I loved her accent, her Eastern European manners. It's just a pity I discovered later that the entire story had been a fabrication. She had spun me all sorts of nonsense about being mistreated – her person violated, in fact, during the course of the conflict in the former Yugoslavia.

– I no fadder, mudder, was one of her favourite lines.

Which apparently was intended to mean:

– I do not have any surviving parents.

Subsequently established, with deep regret, as the most appallingly self-serving of falsehoods.

I confronted her, obviously. She pleaded, in her counter-feit abject fashion.

– I'm suh-sorry, dear, I said and could not find it within me to relent.

Confining her to her room for a period of one week.

I have no doubt, of course, but that Dr Thornton would have approved. I remember smiling, indulging myself in the fancy that I heard him musing in the firelight:

– A firm hand is essential, my boy. Subordinate your emotions to your will and you'll survive. Excellent show – I have to say I'm impressed. At last you're doing something of which I can be proud. Backbone. Mettle! That's you, my boy! Christopher Thornton, at last that's become your name! Indifferent, incurious, self-controlled but best of all decisive! Unlike our friends who are of a degraded and inferior status. And you know, my boy, of whom I speak.

Madame Vesna Krapotnik had told me all sorts of wonderful things about Dubrovnik. About how she had been born in the district of the old town, which was like something out of a medieval painting, with its mosaics, Gothic cathedrals and marble architecture. I continued to remain completely in her power as she described the fascinating magic of the coastal city, where she had been born twenty-eight years before.

– It sounds so special, I said, almost holy.

– It is, she said. Dubrovnik is holy. Is the place where I was born, liff all my life.

Except that she happened not to be born there at all, but in some godforsaken dump of a fishing village, which no one had ever heard of.

But she had looked so beautiful that day, with those small blonde curls peeping out from underneath the pale-blue patterned scarf that framed her fresh, blue-eyed complexion, as I rested my chin on my meerschaum cane, staring at her, smiling as she told me all about her father, who was a sheet-metal worker who had been wounded in the war, and her mother, who had written poetry extolling the beauties of Dubrovnik. That very first day in the café on the Plaza, hours just seemed to keep drifting on by, and it was like I had become so talkative we might have been back in the sixties again.

Obviously I couldn't tell her anything about St Catherine's, I had no intention of scaring the girl off. Not that I got all that much of an opportunity, to be honest, after she got over her initial shyness. As they used to say in the old days, that girl would have talked the hind legs off a donkey. There was a lovely little mannerism she had that I particularly liked, of leaning forward to stroke her knee, as her little nose puckered. She had been educated by nuns, she told me, but wasn't really what you would call a practising Catholic any longer, having seen at close hand what religion could do to people. Yes, I replied, we've had it here too, Vesna, believe me, but thankfully, as you say, it's all over. People should just accept each other for what they are, she suggested, and went on to tell me that she loved Cat Stevens.

– *Mona Bone Jakon*, she said and just for a minute I thought it was Croatian she was speaking. But it turned out to be Cat Stevens' first album.

– I really like so much, she said, his beautiful moosik. And Gordon Lightfoot and Carole King, yes – very much.

I liked those too, I informed this wonderful new lady in my life, but preferred easy listening. Which, I'm delighted to be able to say, she was also overjoyed to hear, for she liked it too, Tony Bennett in particular. We exchanged phone numbers when we had finished our meal and I began to see her quite regularly after that. But the extraordinary thing is, in the beginning I didn't suspect a single thing. I even believed her when she said she was working, acting as a translator in the Croatian Embassy. I believed nearly everything she told me, for heaven's sake, as we strolled arm in arm, like long-time lovers, as I twirled my cane and looked into her eyes.

Privately thinking: There's life in the old dog yet, ladies and gentlemen. *Rave on!*

And could not help thinking that Vesna, with her fair curly locks held in place by her scarf, did not look at all unlike a singer-songwriter of the seventies, herself thoughtful and quite beautiful in her blue Levi's jeans and embroidered halter-neck top. As she continued with her evocative, historical tales. Concerning her 'kaantry' and 'mudder' and 'fadder, yess?' Who had suffered so much but who she longed to go back one day and see. And no doubt, perhaps, give them some of my money – of which, mysteriously, she always seemed to be in need. And was constantly promising to return.

Vesna Krapotnik, cutest little fibber in all of Croatia. Vesna Krapotnik, so-called exploited refugee, who'd have bled me for all she could if she'd been able. If I hadn't wised up before it was too late. Thank you, virtual highway, and *Perfidia.com*. But, most of all, thank you to my natural instincts, which in spite of all didn't fail me in the end.

– Vuh-vuh-Vesna, luh-luh big liar! I said to myself when I found out.

That she'd been working as a cleaner in a restaurant, and had never been inside the Croatian Embassy in her life.

But that as yet was a little way away.

17   The Beachcomber Affair

That day I waited at the corner to meet Marcus – it's my greatest regret. I ought never to have done it. But at least, now that a great deal of time has elapsed, I can appreciate that it was my own absurd degree of emotionalism and naivety which was responsible for the resulting calamity.

No, I should never have invested Marcus Otoyo with such impossible qualities. Qualities which, in fact, had never existed. Marcus was nothing more than an ordinary youth going through a phase – exactly as Mossie Phelan had suggested.

It was inevitable that he'd grow up and I ought to have been aware of that: that, even as we talked that day in the street, he was already in the process of leaving what remained of his childhood behind. Something Evelyn Dooris couldn't have been expected to understand – being scarcely thirteen. Which only tends to add to one's sympathy for her. For there could be no doubting her disappointment that day in the greenhouse. Her soul was cast down – you could tell that immediately. Unaware, perhaps, that she too was entering a new period in her life, and that soon her schooldays also would be but a memory. Like those of Marcus Otoyo – except that my myopia of hopeless belief and longing had blinded me to the fact.

The progression of events seems so stunningly simple now – something which comforts me in my advancing years. I had desired, more than anything, to be comparably spiritual, to share somehow in Marcus's extraordinarily pious passions – those I had assumed to be burning deep within him. To be permitted to scale the foothills and crest the dizzying heights, where, my imagination had told me, destiny had placed him. And from whence he gazed down haughtily, upon the insignificant plod of the dismal human herd. In his image and likeness, I would secure the adoration and respect I had so long been denied, I felt certain.

From the very first night I'd seen myself standing outside the Thornton Manor house with its high French windows, gazing in at my mother Lady Thornton, who was little more than a blur as she turned the pages of the golden treasury, reading, as always, to her beloved Little Tristram. Who lay there, luxuriously, desultorily, with his thumb in his mouth, curled up cosily in her warm lap. At one with her and everything about him. *Inside*, I thought. *Belonging*.

On the very first page of *A Child's Garden of Verses* – the most beautiful book in the world – there was an ink drawing of an ancient crumbling portal, whose pillars were twined with leaves. And then, underneath, in ornate script, a sentence which read: *Enter through here and inherit human happiness. Abide with us herein beneath the stars of the bluest heaven.*

I really don't think that, even if I had wanted to, I could have prevented myself from visiting Ethel that day. Because of my memories of her and that book. But I was wasting my time, as I realise now, searching for something she would always have found it impossible to give. She hadn't a clue what I meant, poor woman, pestering her about 'this holy city we call love', and all the rest of it. Prevailing upon her to read 'Escape at Bedtime', in particular. Yes, she remembered the book, she told me – but only vaguely. So it had been a pointless exercise, emulating Tristram – manoeuvring myself into her lap, I mean. And which had been so awkward, for both of us. I should never have requested that. For, as has been reasonably, if I'm honest, suggested, it was my very insistence that had been primarily responsible for her cardiac arrest.

But I sometimes think, even yet, and in spite of myself, I'll often find myself thinking: If only she *had* been capable of understanding. It could have been so beautiful, almost as good as the way I'd dreamed it, with at long last the French windows of Thornton Manor slowly parting – and Lady Thornton approaching me with arms outspread, crying joyfully:

– But of course you can enter your own house, my dear boy.

But it wasn't to be.

I suppose it's true to say that, at the ripe old age of sixty-seven, C.J. Pops, ancient husky relic of the good old sixties, has, if nothing else, succeeded at last in growing up. But not only that, has also discovered the secret of endurance and survival. That which comes of pledging fealty to but one single creed, that very same one which now like a cleansing fog spreads out across Western Europe, desultorily floating across the flagstones of the Plaza, where the pudding-faced families repose, as ever, beneath the patiently revolving screens. Attired in their loose-fitting leisurewear, mutely passing wine across the table as one turns, with a single head, smooth and round as a consecrated bread, now facing in my direction – bold escutcheon of this rational new epoch, ephemeral cipher, neat round rubric formed with a chilling, perfect artistry. Regarding me eerily, the starkest orb:

0

As perfectly formed as a consecrated bread.

I can't say for sure just how long exactly I had been going with Dolores McCausland when I found myself waking up one night in the Nook, with – to my astonishment – the following words thrusting from my mouth:

– *Marcus Otoyo, hear this call. Appease for me the longings of my heart, will you?*

I didn't sleep for the remainder of the night. Kept tossing and turning and experiencing perplexing, near-feverish visions. One of which in particular was most frightening in its realism. I could almost hear the clamour in the room: that same disjointed cacophony the soldiers might have made in their grim approach to Gethsemane. A detachment of guards – led by Marcus, all bearing lanterns and torches and weapons. I was standing there alone when I saw him at the gate.

– We have crossed the Kedron Valley to come here, he said, and whispered:

– The one that I shall kiss – that is he.

Then he smiled with those gleaming eyes and I could feel a warm tear beginning to steal down my cheek.

It was only a day later, the moment I saw him outside the Five Star supermarket, that jarringly, almost immediately, the same sentence entered my mind: The one that I shall kiss: that is he.

I involuntarily flinched as it did so, edging into an alleyway as he passed.

But, generally speaking, that episode would have proved an exception around then. Most of the time it was delightful, to be honest. To employ the period parlance, we were having ourselves an absolute ball. Dolly and I had never got along better, and we were the talk of the place as we zoomed around in my E-Type substitute. As we went *vroom!* in the town of Cullymore. Cue *Bullitt*, by Lalo Schifrin. You got it, Pops, it's outasite. No, I jest. I may not really have been a sixties superstar like Ray Davies, or John Lennon, or Sean Connery, for that matter, but as far as anyone from Cullymore was concerned, Chris McCool, he sure was turning out to be a pretty 'cool mover'. A regular up-to-the-minute outatown hep cat and no mistake.

*   *   *

Emboldened by Dolly's continued encouragement, I worked on refining my image somewhat, to the extent that it wasn't David Hemmings I resembled so much any longer, instead with my thick bushy moustache I looked every inch the twin of Peter Sarstedt, the medallion-sporting singer with shiny boots and crushed-velvet pants. And whose massive hit 'Where Do You Go To My Lovely' was to be heard almost everywhere throughout that summer.

Along with my impressive facial hair, I was sporting a nice blow-dry hairstyle now, set and styled in the fashion of the time, and tending, in dress, to favour ribbed polos in a variety of bright colours, along with high-waisted flared bell-bottoms. I couldn't have been happier. Why not, for heaven's sake? With Dolly now openly referring to me as 'her hunk'. Her very own Mr Wonderful, she would proudly say.

'Toot! Toot!' would go the horn as I picked her up every evening at the house in Wattles Lane, to take her down for a drink in the Good Times. Sometimes I'd see Marcus sitting by the window of his bedroom, studying.

As was my wont at that time, of course, and with no evidence, I remained convinced that it was *A Portrait* he was reading. And it affected me, obviously. Wrenched me, in fact. The emotions I experienced best described by its author within those very pages: *Wounded pride and fallen hope and baffled desire.*

It was on account of those inexplicable surges of feeling that I would find myself, falteringly, beginning to make the most unnecessary, unconvincing excuses.

– I don't think I'll be able to go down to Wattles Lane tonight, Dolly. I'm really sorry. I have accounts to do. I have three supermarkets to deliver eggs to tomorrow.

But somehow she always succeeded, in the end, in persuading me. And before I knew it we'd be sitting there chatting away to Marcus's mother, as he himself continued with his studies in the other room – preparing arduously for the forthcoming play, *The Soul's Ascent: Saints You May Not Know*. Every time I went down now, he seemed to be there: ensconced in the same place – frowning intensely, wholly absorbed. Assimilating every possible scrap of knowledge about the saints of old, their magnificent visions and selfless sacrifices. I noticed a booklet lying on the table. *The Blessed Martin de Porres Story*, it was called. As I say, being of colour, Marcus had specifically been chosen for the part. *The Soul's Ascent: Saints You May Not Know* in part examined the life of Martin de Porres.

– I'm so lucky, I had overheard him saying to his mother, so lucky to have been chosen. For Blessed Martin is my favourite saint of all.

I found myself charmed, utterly disarmed by his manner and by the spontaneity of this admission. There was something so open-hearted and all-embracing about his youthful tolerance, his belief in all peoples.

In the beginning, of course, and which I understand now, what I ought to have done was to laugh dismissively whenever Dolly told her Marcus Otoyo stories.

– He really does think he's a saint, silly boy! Those daft old Catholic books, filling his head with nonsense! But he does make me howl, I have to say. You should have seen his face the day I was ironing my petticoat. The eyes, I swear, nearly popped out of his head. So amusing.

Sometimes, very occasionally, I might have enjoyed her telling those stories. But other times I would resent it – finding it increasingly difficult to conceal my irritation.

As she whinnied with laughter and primped her permed hair.

– One day, just for a giggle, don't you know, I read a little bit to him from *Titbits* magazine, Chris. You should have seen his innocent blushes!

I couldn't believe the sudden harshness of my voice. The chalk-white aspect of my expression, my clenched fists.

– *That's disgusting! Do you really have to humiliate him in such a fashion? Is that the way all Protestants must behave? Is it absolutely necessary?*

Why had such thoughts even entered my head? I was flummoxed.

I remember Dolly looking pale and quite shocked. She had actually left the Nook early that evening, even after I'd tried to placate her.

– No, Chris, I have to go, Chris, she kept saying – appearing very disconcerted indeed.

And the way she looked at me, just before she left. It was as if what she was thinking was: He's a Catholic all right. Prone to bouts of shame and quite irrational, disturbing violence. A Catholic to his very bones. Vitiated, profligate – lacking sobriety and self-control. He simply doesn't possess the neutrality of the Protestant – the coolness, the distance.

Spiritually infirm, bereft of the capacity to subordinate emotion. Impartiality is alien to him.

But I could have been imagining that. As Mossie used to say:

– For certain souls of a more sensitive nature, the embrace of Catholicism can sometimes prove a disaster – its excesses encouraging paranoia and delusions, often extreme and sharpened heights of perception. Over-sensitivity ought not, in certain cases, to be encouraged, for it can be potentially devastating. But only for certain unfortunates, you do understand.

He's right. But thankfully now, that's all consigned to the dustbin of the past. Catholicism and everything to do with it removed now as though they never existed. As peace reigns supreme along the Plaza and in the Happy Club. C. J. Pops and his babe, Vesna Krapotnik.

A time to be born, this balloon-headed time – a unique era of stability and opportunity. Where we all, with eager willingness, are dutiful zeros. With our life paths signposted upon a virtual highway. The bleached calm of the twenty-first century. Never has such harmony existed in history, or so the vox pops repeatedly tell us. Of course, as usual, not everyone is in accord with this appraisal. The media remain preoccupied with the debate and there is endless speculation about the disappearance of certain values and rules. The rise in suicide being attributed to the collapse of the well-tried framework of Western civilisation. Annihilation of consciousness appears now to be the norm, it is routinely suggested.

And which, if it is true – and I'm inclined to think it is – then, believe me, is a development that causes me no discomfort at all. Quite the opposite, in fact. Having willingly dispensed with my own ego some time ago. Enlisting in the ranks of the pudding-faces myself, or as Mike prefers, the good old Eggmen. The mute serried lines of ghostly coins. Knowing only too well that I might never have survived if I didn't. Survived to become 'Old Pops' here in the apartments – yep, C.J. McCool, Ambassador of the Void: retired swinger, former tenant of the salubrious White Room. Now as insignificant and untroubled as every other drained and grateful cipher. Which is amusing, of course, for back in the old days, quite coincidentally, they used to casually refer to me as 'the Eggman'.

Although, obviously, of course, for entirely different reasons.

No, I'm a nouveau Eggman in this clean new century, this world of white wax – and which is exactly the way I desire it. In order that I might continue to remain anonymous, to abide in a world of weightless, floating orbs – pathologically incurious as to the welfare of one's fellows. As we pass the wine across the table once more – unmoved, detached, attired in our shapeless, brightly coloured loungewear, our smooth round faces free of any blemish, with no end to the spoils now placed at our disposal. For all the world indeed, like rows of eggs neatly stacked in trays. Just as I used to arrange them when bringing them to the Five Star, one by one in their cardboard trays. For the most part dutiful and mute, perfectly formed little objects: until sometimes, for no reason, you'd get it into your head that, somehow, something was inexpressibly wrong – seeing them then as something quite different. Terrified mouths, frozen silence, crying out from the limbo's maw.

'They Are the Eggmen!' Mike always starts to strum as soon as he sees me arriving into Mood Indigo. Then, after that, 'No Milk Today' by Herman's Hermits, that hopelessly buoyant almost ludicrously happy melody which seems to encapsulate the very essence of the sixties. That cheeky, optimistic bubblegum whimsy which seems the definitive mood of that time.

Although, sometimes, to be honest – whenever I'm feeling under the weather – I could get along just as well without Mike and his happy tunes. However, I'd never dream of saying that to him. He doesn't need to know things like that. Or the reason I sometimes shiver whenever he plays 'No Milk Today' is that it happened to be playing on Evelyn's transistor that day when I made my way to meet Marcus, at their little greenhouse, the Holy of Holies. Which is where I'd hoped to find him – in order to clear up our little misunderstanding, put it behind us once and for all.

I had been hiding behind some bushes watching Evelyn. She was busying herself now, having been praying for some time. When I decided at last to make an appearance, she didn't seem at all taken aback – just carried on arranging some flowers. My throat was dry and hoarse as I said:

– I'm sorry, Evelyn: I thought I might find him here – Marcus Otoyo, I mean.

– No, she replied, I'm afraid he won't be coming out here any more. He said if I want I can throw his things away.

– Throw them away?

– His posters and that. His pictures. All his various bits and pieces.

She seemed sad when she was saying it.

There was a framed oleograph of Blessed Martin de Porres mounted directly above her head, with his two hands joined as he lifted his curly ebony head up to heaven. Just for a moment, it raised my spirits. When I thought of just how extraordinary his performance had been in the play, *The Soul's Ascent*. But then I looked at Evelyn and, dismayed, instantly appreciated the situation: in fact, her downcast eyes told their own story. I knew now if I waited I would only be wasting my time.

He wasn't coming. He wouldn't *be* coming.

Which I ought to have known. The sharp exchange which had taken place between us only an hour or two before ought to have taught me that much.

– He's too grown-up now, she told me ruefully, before looking away. He says it's just for kids, all this. It's over. Whether it's sad or not, it's over. It's done.

*   *   *

After she left, an all-pervasive gloominess began to descend on me and my limbs assumed the most terrible weight. Tucking Robert Louis Stevenson's golden treasury under my arm, as I took a final look at the greenhouse before departing myself.

All the way back into town I found myself utterly distraught and all I could think of were lines from mythology, commingling with those from the golden treasury: No, we cannot abide in the city of fallen hope. There will be no peace in that place where hope and love have been seen to die. It is a city unholy, and deserves to be destroyed, its gates torn down, its temples razed.

It was a difficult and emotional time, and who in their right mind would want to revisit it? One is undoubtedly infinitely better off, in these, the white-world days. Where one is sustained by systematic, clean-washed *numbness*. A platinum anaesthesia.

Not only reassuring – but also, as I have found recently, so *convenient*. I mean – consider that urchin to whom, only recently, I administered the beating – richly deserved, might I say. Once upon a time it would have been considered impossible, indeed hopelessly so, certainly in a small country like Ireland, for such an incident to occur with no significant investigation taking place, indeed with no seeming consequences at all ensuing. Which, as I say happily for me, proved to be the case. Why, the brat probably hadn't even bothered to report the incident. Fearful, no doubt, that he might end up like that other little fool I once read about in the paper, another little Sambo who had been brought back to an apartment – only to find himself eaten by his host, the cannibal Jeffrey Dahmer. Returned there, can you believe it, by the very same policemen to whom he had appealed for assistance.

Yes, like everywhere else, from New York to LA, London to Dubai, it seems rootless strays just come and go now with the weather, as do refugees of all shapes and hues, littering the Plaza like so much human junk. And I cannot help but think that Henry Thornton would have approved: of its essential indifference to emotion but also its judicious self-control and order – empirical, non-spiritual, with all un-essential emotion systematically siphoned.

– Incurious, he'd have smiled, yes, an impartiality to which I give my blessing. For it seems to me that in the current times the *ancien* code has been rehabilitated. The mystery of Protestantism. The need for order never dies, and so they must deliver themselves into the infinitely more capable hands of their superiors. Who, by birth and instinct, are obviously sovereign, autonomous and self-contained.

The best thing I could have done, I suppose, in the circumstances, would have been to finish with Dolores – and to do it resolutely: honestly and cleanly. But I couldn't, for the life of me, seem to find the opportunity. In spite of our disagreement, she continued calling out to the Nook. I suppose the reason for my hesitancy being the fact that I liked her so much – maybe in my own way even loved Dolly Mixtures. One thing for sure, I will never forget what her parting words were to me, that so sad day when we met for the final time.

When I ran into her by accident in one of the aisles of the Five Star.

– You're devious, do you know that? she said to me coldly. I realise now that I haven't known the first thing about you.

That was what she had said – *to me*! When the truth was, in fact – as far as I was concerned – that it was the other way round.

Like all excursions to Butlin's Holiday Camps in those more unassuming times, that day in 1969 bore all the prospects of being something close to a visit to some kind of replica heaven. Which was always, of course, how it had seemed in the brochures: as a kind of miniature paradise, full of bold and brash, startling wonders. A pocket universe glimpsed through a knothole. *Our true intent is all for your delight*, read the greeting arched regally above the camp entrance, flickering in pink and blue soft neon. You wanted to cry out, and proclaim the uniqueness of its marvels to all. But you couldn't – you just gasped. And continued feasting your eyes upon the giant white cockerels strutting by the side of the boating lake and the glass-walled lounge that was lit in bright orange, as zebra-striped fish looped sleepily behind glass panels. With the monorail swooping and diving and the massive plants in acid greens adorning its shiny-squared mezzanines and terraces, what met our eyes might well have been a vision of the future.

But the highlight of that visit, I'm afraid, proved to be none of these particular phantasmagoric delights, or the long hours spent on the dodgems and fairground rides. But that dreadful night when I found myself falling out into the night, after I'd quit the Beachcomber Bar, where Dolly had been working her way through her repertoire, enthralling the audience as per usual. It was an appalling business, the Beachcomber Affair, not, as I liked to joke to myself about it later, like some amusingly light-hearted episode from the television series *The Man from Uncle* but an occurrence which succeeded in debilitating me to a truly distressing degree and for which, even yet, I find it difficult to find the words. No, the Beachcomber Affair was anything but amusing, or light-hearted either. In that the affair which took place that night in Butlin's of Mosney – it was just about as real as it could get.

The Beachcomber Bar, with its clam-shell stage and papier mâché models of Easter Island stone faces, its palm fronds and fish nets, rattan ceiling, Polynesian carvings and wicker chairs, was packed to the door with enthusiastic dancers – practically every night of the week.

The Vince Broy Band were performing on this occasion – hilariously, from the audience's point of view, attired in grass skirts and garlands of flowers. Playing, as their programme had promised, 'all the summer's fantabulous hits'.

Ever since my 'Catholic' emotional outburst, I had become insecure – quite edgy now, in Dolly's company. And, as I sat there nursing my coloured 'Rainbow Bird' cocktail, staring, preoccupied, at the cornucopia of thick coloured glass bottles suspended from the ceiling, I could not prevent myself from perspiring heavily. And rerunning all of her stories in my mind. All of the 'little encounters' she'd told me about, regarding Marcus. The *News of the World. Hospitals' Requests. Dear Frankie.* Marcus Minor, I'd think, and, simultaneously: The holy place: love's ancient city.

I was at my wits' end, frankly. Thinking of him laughing as he reached out to touch her hand, saying:

– Ariadne, my precious. I, Marcus Otoyo, upon this orphan earth, am and shall remain your sole appointed envoy.

Quite cleverly, even cruelly, it began to appear to me now, as I sat there trying to prevent the drink from quivering in my hand, dressed up as nothing of any greater importance than whimsy:

– *Dear Frankie, my boyfriend is a very puritanical man. He will not permit me to wear tights or jewellery.*

Each tale delivered as if it were of no import: frivolous, disposable gossip – nothing more, nothing less. But the more I turned them all over in my mind – she had only just started up 'Mr Wonderful' now – the more I became convinced of exactly what it meant.

Why, Dolly, I inwardly pleaded, why Marcus?

Why indeed. As I looked down to see that two of my fingers were, in fact, bleeding and that the stem of the glass had broken off in my hand.

*   *   *

To this day I cannot determine for sure exactly what length of time had elapsed after I had removed myself from the bar that night, quite intoxicated, I regret to say. I waited for quite some time but now there were only a few minutes remaining before a shocking and truly traumatic sight was to meet my eyes. An encounter which, quite irrevocably, was on the verge of changing everything in my life. But which, in a way, I had been half expecting.

I heard the murmur of voices first: muffled, furtive – not that that was any surprise. But then, quite startlingly – a sudden peal of girlish laughter. As I approached chalet number 11, the rickety clapboard cabin where Marcus was supposed to have been residing alone. That was the arrangement. The one condition that of course – laughably, in retrospect – had been 'laid down' by his mother.

After hearing a ripple of the laughter again, I mustered what pitiful reserves of courage remained to me, galvanising myself to peer through the grubby panes of the chalet window, a tautness gathering in my chest that grew close to unbearable. But not even my worst imaginings could have prepared me for what was about to transpire.

Marcus Otoyo was standing in semi-darkness now, bathed in the light of the moon, splendidly attired in a neatly pressed suit. As Dolores ran her fingers along his thin tie, he might have been an absurdly youthful and quite urbane city gentleman. The black suit was neatly cut with narrow, sharp lapels.

Peggy Lee was playing very softly in the background as Dolores McCausland continued staring into his eyes, pressing her lips to his ear as she whispered:

– Tell me, Mr Wonderful. Do you love me?

Then she began, quite methodically, tenderly and patiently, to remove each item of his clothing – it was abundantly clear that this was not the first time that had happened – placing tiny pecks, soft kisses on his chest.

I thrust my knuckles against my clenched teeth and cried out:

– *Vile betrayer! Treacherous Judas! Love's holy city, it falls now into sand!*

That's all I can remember for the remainder of that night. Apart from the door of my chalet opening – some two hours later – and Dolly, with a fur coat draped over her frosted-pink Dreamland nightdress, whispering:

– Are you awake, Mr Wonderful? I hope you were expecting me to pay you a visit, were you?

I subsequently began studiously avoiding Wattles Lane. His mother would often stop me in the Five Star or on the street to enquire as to whether there was a problem of some kind. I said why of course not, of course there isn't a problem. As she said but our eggs and you've not delivered any buttermilk, not for at least three weeks now past. No, I said, I'm up to my eyes. The supermarkets can't get enough these days, what with the way business is going in the town.

But I could tell the excuse wasn't very convincing.

– You look pale, she said. If you like I can send Marcus out to get it. Out to the farm, I mean.

My response was foolish, falsetto, practically:

– *No! Do you hear me!*

I routinely wept now – uncontrollably, to be honest, entirely unmanned by wounded pride and baffled desire.

Whenever I turned on the radio it was never Herman's Hermits or the Animals now. It always seemed to be Stevie Wonder – unabashedly proclaiming his love for his *Cherie Amour, lovely as a summer's day . . . distant as the Milky Way.* I grew to loathe it more than anything. More than anything I grew to despise that song.

And would find myself saying, my eyes smarting with anger and confusion and bitterness as I did so:

– Don't ever trust any of them. Niggers, they're notorious.

Why, I might have been Dr Henry Thornton, I laughed. Before weeping and chafing my knuckles again.

I tended not to sleep very much now. I didn't care much for the dances either. Slowly but surely the effect it all had on me was that I began to hate the times that I lived in, to loathe the decade I lived in called 'the sixties'. And loathe it with a passion, despise it with all my heart. To hate who I was and what I had become.

How I wished I'd come of age in the twenties or the thirties. Even the threadbare fifties would have been better.

Infinitely so. But much much better than any of them, I now found myself considering on a regular basis – would never to have been conceived at all. As a half-Protestant bastard, in a barn or anywhere else.

Once when I happened to arrive home unexpectedly to the apartment, to my astonishment what did I discover, only Vesna doing a little private dance in the flat and playing a CD with a Lulu track on it – 'To Sir With Love', as a matter of fact. I flew across the room and straight away tore the music-system plug right out of its socket. Then I wrenched the CD case from her hand. I gave her what for after that, I can tell you – I mean I had to, actually at one point pushing her down on to the sofa and lifting my meerschaum cane, on the verge of giving her a proper thrashing. But, as might have been expected, she hadn't the faintest clue what I was talking about, poor thing. How could she? She didn't even know who Sidney Poitier was, for heaven's sake. Much less be aware that he had co-starred in a feature film with Lulu, and which, in fact, had been a big hit back in the year 1969.

– I'm sorry, I said later. I didn't mean it.

I was still trembling violently. As Vesna gave me the puppy-eye look – Lord but she was good at that – nervously fingering the necklace I had given her as a present, some weeks before.

– I no understand iss just song, no?

I didn't say anything. I couldn't speak. The skeleton of the melody was still lingering in my ears.

– Lulu, I kept thinking, with uneasy tingles spreading all over my back, *Lulu.*

As I scratched my head and obsessively paced the room. Repeating:

– Luh-luh-Lulu. Luh-luh-Lulu.

With her twirly red hair and lovely baby dimples.

– Luh-luh-Lulu, I kept on saying, as Vesna sobbed, begging forgiveness all over again.

I held up my walking cane and considered for a moment – then I simply put it away.

It was late March now, 1969, and it would soon be time for the play in the cathedral. There were posters for *The Soul's Ascent* pasted up everywhere.

But all that did now was fill me with bitterness. I no longer wanted to think about him or his part in a stupid and inconsequential amateur school play, which, at the end of the day, was all it was. More than anything, I disdained talk of the soul, and in particular the possibility of its 'ascent'.

I wished I had never laid eyes on Joyce's *Portrait.* But one sentence, in particular, kept returning with a fierce aggression to my mind: *amid the tumult of wounded pride and fallen hope and baffled desire, a film of sorrow veiled his eyes.*

– You stupid little tabernacle of Christ, I moaned. What you have done to me.

If I heard Stevie Wonder on the radio, I'd fly into an inexplicable rage. Even the sight of *A Portrait* now had the effect of making me feel queasy.

I had tried telling Dolly I wouldn't be seeing her any more.

She was aghast, she told me – quite astonished.

– No, Mr Wonderful, tell me anything but please don't tell me that, she implored.

– My name isn't Mr Wonderful, I said, without feeling.

– You don't realise what you're saying. Please say it's a joke: is it, Mr Wonderful?

I found myself growing cold all over. Yet again, becoming so cold – only this time without realising it – I might have been Henry Thornton.

– I told you my name is not Mr Wonderful, I said.

She looked at me then – drawing back a little – quite afraid now, it seemed.

– It was you who took the envelope, wasn't it? You stole that letter out of my handbag.

I didn't say anything.

As her lower lip began to tremble.

– Now I see, she said, haltingly, reluctantly. It's not me you care about at all, is it? Oh my God.

– There's nothing further to say, I told her.

She dropped some things out of her handbag as she turned to go.

– Dolly! I called after her.

– Get away from me. Stay away – do you hear?

Yes, C.J. Pops, 'real gone' grooving sixties freak. Just how would you describe what really was 'his bag'?

By this point now, the performance in the cathedral had begun to draw near. Everywhere you went there were conversations about it, with printed additions to the posters confidently predicting it would be the 'event of the year'.

The Soul's Ascent: Saints You May Not Know, starring Marcus Otoyo as Blessed Martin de Porres. There was a photo of him with a white halo set in place just behind his head: as he smiled faintly with folded hands and uplifted eyes, in his habit of brown and girdle of beads. Like an angel on the verge of ascending to heaven. To announce the establishment of the long-awaited 'new Jerusalem'.

– The holy city, I repeated, grinding my teeth. The holy city of love gone wrong.

19   A Walk in the Black Forest

It's funny when you look back on things sometimes but if I had thought that the episode with 'Dr Mukti the Midget' had been amusing, it was nothing to what took place only a few nights after the Beachcomber Affair. I had been away all day getting the 'E-Type' serviced in Dublin and was exhausted by the time I got back to the Nook. So just about the last thing I was expecting to hear when I came in the door was music.

Especially music by Herb Alpert and his band. But there they were, delivering 'Tijuana Taxi', in full flight. The sound appeared to be coming from the kitchen. I tiptoed tensely along the hallway. And sure enough, there they were. Not paying the slightest attention to me, I have to say, in their neatly tailored blazers and ribbed white-nylon polo necks.

Perched, almost treacherously, on the rim of a drinking glass. Surprising as it was, what could you possibly do but laugh? I hadn't even had anything to drink.

Bemused, I shook my head somewhat wearily before retiring to bed, with the next tune they'd just started already playing on my lips: 'A Walk in the Black Forest', a perky upbeat jazz number, once again delivered in Herb's trademark mariachi style.

20   City of Sapphire

Probably the finest band I have ever seen playing in a pub –
anywhere, I would have to say – is the group of youngsters,
not one of them, I would say, over twenty, who deputise
occasionally for Mike and the Chordettes in the Mood
Indigo club and who style themselves (this 'retro' thing
remains ever-popular) after a famous combo from the sixties
– Dave Dee, Dozy, Beaky, Mick and Tich. Who were a very
well-known outfit indeed, throughout the course of their
career chalking up a considerable batch of hits. Numbers
which included 'Hold Tight', 'The Legend of Xanadu' and,
of course, 'Zabadak'.

Another much-requested act is the Engelbert Humperdinck lookalike who always gets the crowd going whenever
he appears, complete with gold medallion and impossibly
hirsute sideburns.

Vesna liked him a lot too, and would flutter her thick
black lashes at me as she cooed:

– You like me dance, Christopher my dear? You think iss
good idea, hmm?

In the beginning she winced at the idea of me making
suggestions – as to how she might dress, I mean. But
whenever she got into it – I mean, on any given night

in the club you'd find at least two Dusty Springfields – she began to rather enjoy the idea. 'Peggy Lee', I'd whisper, or 'Ruby Murray' – as I squeezed her hand and kissed her lacquered blonde hair. By the time I was finished with her all trace of the seventies songwriter was gone, with the flared blue jeans discarded for ever. The same with the trendy peasant-style scarf and halter-neck top, now in their place spray-on sheath dresses and panda eyes, and expensive high heels that I bought for her on eBay. Which she dandled on her pretty foot as she sat beside me holding my hand, moving her lips in time to the music.

While I whispered:

– Miss Wonderful, it's you, and her body would vibrate with the loveliest little ripple of delight.

Yes, we made quite a couple and, more than anyone, Vesna Krapotnik from Croatia knew it. It's just a pity she had to go and spoil it, but there isn't anything that can be done about that now. We looked good dancing together too. And, just as he had once done in the Mayflower of yesteryear, old Roger McCool-Moore, alias 'the Saint', would never pass up an opportunity to demonstrate his considerable ballroom-dancing skills – his cha-cha, his tango and his quickstep, Mr Twinkletoes the hoofer in his white Italian loafers, a Peter Stuyvesant, as ever, dangling louchely from his lips – *the international passport to smoking pleasure*!

As he twirled his meerschaum cane with a smile.

*　　　*　　　*

Maybe the fact that I no longer bother going down to the club, now that I have more or less lost interest in going to Mood Indigo, is the ultimate indication that, at last, it has happened. That I have been cured, once and for all. And no longer feel the need to make an impression of any kind on anyone. Being capable of just being myself, content to live my life here with Vesna in the blissful tranquillity of the Happy Club. It helps, of course, that her affections are no longer in any doubt, for no relationship can withstand unremitting uncertainty and suspicion. In a way I like to think of our new-found contentment as a kind of brand-new version of 'the Nook', on those nights when Ethel and my mother would arrive, under cover of darkness, bearing gifts. With one present, as always, standing out in my mind: that little golden treasury, *A Child's Garden of Verses*, by Robert Louis Stevenson. From which I continue to derive unlimited pleasure, turning its pages each night in the Happy Club, here in our love-nest. Sucking my thumb as I stare at the sky, where my old friends the stars wink back in approval – Joyce's blue fruit of heaven: Orion and Cassiopeia, and the infinite majesty of the Milky Way.

A life which we have been living for well over the best part of a year now. And one which, at least once upon a time, I would have considered impossible – quite literally unattainable. How wrong I was.

But back then, of course, things were immeasurably different. Yes, a year or so ago the relationship between

Vesna and me, well, it had not been going so good at all. There was no such thing as the Happy Club then. Which is hardly surprising – after all, I had caught her in the act of stealing from me. Sometimes, even yet – I get the eeriest of feelings whenever I think about it. Especially whenever I'm crossing the Plaza, passing the café where we two first met. It's a strange, hollowed-out, empty kind of sensation. And I must emphasise that I really don't like it. I don't like recalling catching my wife in the act, what husband would. I call Vesna 'my wife', although strictly speaking, of course, she's not. It's just another of our private little games. We got married, you see, in a 'Happy Club' ceremony, one night when we'd been drinking, and I played – quite convincingly, I have to say! – the role of the priest. Why, I was almost as convincing as Marcus Otoyo!

It remains difficult to believe that one's wife – whom one loves – would pilfer. But that is what happened. And I suppose the fact that I have never really accepted it is where those feelings come from. That sensation I get when crossing the Plaza, especially when I think of her lovely laughter. It's a kind of sickness, similar in nature to that which assailed me when I apprehended her on the landing, brazenly going through my coat pockets. Yes, the grateful lady I'd taken in off the street. That was what she did, I'm afraid. Madame Vesna the rifler. Yes, the much put-upon 'immigrant', who, purportedly, had witnessed so many horrors. Who had somehow, mira-culously, survived the most tragic conflict in Europe since the Second World War. Vesna, poor Vesna: yes, *My fadder die he come bad man and hurt my mudder* etc. etc. Say hello to Vesna Pinocchio, from Dubrovnik in Croatia. Let on, that is.

I remember I had happened to arrive home early that day – as a matter of fact I'd been purchasing some cleaner for my computer – and had known instinctively that something was wrong. I mean, I knew she was there – and was wearing the Chanel No. 5 I'd recently bought her, I could smell it. What I had not expected, however, was this – going through my pockets. Although – I mean I'm not a fool – I'd suspected, and for quite some considerable time – ever since she'd moved into the apartment, in fact – that she'd been stealing from me. Indeed it had recently come to my attention that some items of note had disappeared from my study. And my credit-card outgoings were far in excess of any debt that I, personally, had incurred.

My voice, when I confronted her there in the kitchen, was toneless – rational, authoritative. Almost indifferent.

Very *Henry Thornton*, I am prompted to observe.

The poor girl. Already I knew I had overdone it somewhat. She was, in fact, terrified: sheet-white as she stood there, haplessly dropping coins and other disparate items.

As I eyed her fixedly all along the length of my cane.

That was the night that I finally prised it from her – neither she nor her parents had been involved in the war at all. I sighed resignedly and reassured her that she didn't have to worry.

– I'll do anything, she said, please, Mr Chris.

– Uh-uh-anything? I said, a little embarrassed by my stammering. But, nonetheless, I was determined to press onward.

– Yes, she told me, anything what iss most what you want I will do.

Holding her by the arm – we were standing by the fire – all of a sudden I thought of Henry: his face impassive, ungiving, grave.

– Iniquitous, I muttered gravely. Dissolute.

Before going to a drawer and taking out a tin of black polish. There was a kiwi poking with its beak on the front.

– Here, Vuh-vuh-Vesna, I said, puh-paint your face.

– You don't really want me please, do this.

– You said you'd do anything. So, come along, paint your face. There's a good girl. Thuh-thank you.

When it was over, I don't think I even bothered to smile. She broke down and told me it was crazy.

– Of course it's crazy. It's the sixties, baby, and Stevie Wonder is the star. That's you, *My Cherie Amour* – so get with it, kooks!

But I was wasting my time. She hadn't a clue who Stevie Wonder was.

– Oh forget it, I said, and switched on the television – not bothering to open my mouth for the remainder of the evening.

As she sat there stupidly, not knowing what to do with herself, looking like some idiotic black-and-white minstrel. Making these little occasional pleas for clemency, with her ebony paws sitting there like small birds in her lap. But, like I told her, why should I be in any hurry to forgive her? After all, who was it who had made it come to this?

– I mean, who was the person doing the deceiving, Vesna? I enquired of her coldly a number of times.

And I make no apology for it, for deception is one thing I really do not like. I made no bones about it – it was touch and go if we'd ever live in the Happy Club again. Ever go near it. Fortunately, however, we did in the end, and that unfortunate day now belongs, like a lot of other disagreements between us, to history. Sometimes, even yet, when I see that kiwi on the front of the tin, it always provokes the tiniest little laugh, inducing me to reflect on just how wonderful the Happy Club is, and how lucky we two are, as human beings. Turning the pages of Stevenson once again, as I kiss her softly on the cheek, reciting my favourite verse yet again:

> – They saw me at last, and they chased me with cries,
> And they soon had me packed into bed,
> But the glory kept shining and bright in my eyes,
> And the stars going round in my head.

She looks now as physically attractive as ever she did, Vesna Krapotnik. At least to me. Yes, as beautiful as the day we first met, and that's in spite of the inevitable passage of time. Which, inevitably, in one way or another, affects us all. An inescapable fact of life, and one to which my recent hip replacement will attest. I was worried sick about Vesna all during that fortnight I was forced to spend in hospital. But when I returned, thankfully, everything was exactly as it had been – even down to the golden treasury lying where I'd left it, right beside her on the pillow. The Happy Club, however, needed tidying. Quite a lot of tidying, as I'm sure you can imagine. For with my being away and having no cleaner – it would have caused obvious complications if I'd allowed anyone in – it really was in an appalling state now, so bad that there was actually a rat or two sniffing around, and one of the Moroccan cushions had been torn to pieces.

So it was after that that I set to redecoration with a vengeance. With everything in order – tip-top, in fact. Chic but comfortable, I suppose you might say. And that is the way I intend it to stay, and not just for now or tomorrow. But for as long as Vesna and I remain on this mortal earth. As I luxuriously draw on my Peter Stuyvesant, softly lilting the air of 'We've Only Just Begun' while sitting by the fire, thinking to myself how Vesna Krapotnik is as much a dreamboat now as she was that very first day. When, quite by chance, I encountered her in the café on the Plaza.

So unassailable is our relationship now that we can even laugh and joke about some of the little falsehoods she has perpetrated from time to time.

– You were quite the little minx, weren't you, Madame Vesna – telling me stories about your poor daddy being tortured? Such a silly you must have thought old Popsie! Suh-suh-suh-such a silly you must have thought poor Daddy C.J.!

It's nice to think of the tinkle of her laughter that day as we sat there – for the whole afternoon – sipping our Merlot, and the way she'd lean forward in her blue jeans to stroke her knee, but really and truly she looks so much better now. Certainly much more adventurous in her style of dress. Indeed when I met her, her imagination never seemed to extend beyond the Levi's jeans and peasant-scarf combination, clattering with beads, like something you'd have seen in a folk club in the seventies – a kind of copycat Carole King or Janis Ian, and not too convincing either. But that's all over – binned for ever. And it's sixties glamour for Vesna, all the way.

– *Is that all there is*, Peggy will often sing.

And to which I reply:

– For me it's more than enough, Peggy Lee.

I actually purchase most of her outfits myself: on eBay also. Yes, and take great care doing it, believe me, for the key to creating any image lies in the detail. I have all her items stacked away in the wardrobe, meticulously labelled. Why, it's almost like the Green Shield Stamp shop in there. What with the Dreamland nighties, the pearls, the figure-hugging dresses, the Babushka-style chiffon scarves. There is even a box of Foster Grant sunglasses, the brand of course favoured by Dolores.

I go to all this trouble for the simple reason that nothing – irrespective of any grave transgressions in the past – is good enough now for Vesna Krapotnik. I want to ensure that she really looks smashing. 'A doll', as they used to say way back in the good old you-know-whats.

As I rest my chin upon my walking cane and gaze at her, admiringly: with the mood between us implacable, unmoving – uniquely tranquil.

With not the slightest trace of emotion evident as I calmly lift a nylon stocking from the back of a chair and say:

– There's a good girl, come along now, Vesna, lifting her leg to help put it on.

Stroking her cool forehead – like I say, my own private Kim Novak – as she looks at me tenderly again and smiles. Approvingly, it seems to me, as I turn up the volume, clasping her cold hand as we do our little dance.

Before I smile, as always, and say:

– It's more than enough for me, Peggy Lee.

How heads, I often think, used to turn whenever the two of us would arrive at the club, laughing and joking as we came in the door, with Vesna in her leopardskin cape and me in my Crombie and expensive leather driving gloves. There was something quite showbizzy, really, about the manner in which we disported ourselves. But especially Vesna, my delectable *squeeze*, as they say in cheap novels, having been expertly tutored by myself in the fine arts of fashion and deportment, with assistance from my ever-growing stack of magazines and videos. I had effectively transformed her from dowdy old milkmaid Carole King into a voluptuous supper-club glamourpuss – had swapped the dingy student-bar ambience that her appearance had for so long suggested for the wicked diva-sheen of the *demi-monde*. With not a hair out of place in her lacquered helmet of dyed blonde hair, and her painted pink lips quite out of this world: *soft enough to be innocent, sweet enough to inspire*, as Dolly used to say.

Her image now is more or less complete, and it will rarely deviate from the established routine, which is generally sixties-themed. Her dress can vary, though. Sometimes it will be a simple A-line creation or a cocktail-style figure-hugging dress, but what always remains consistent is its closeness to the style embraced by Dolores McCausland, yes, my old friend Dolly Mixtures, with whom, regrettably, it was fated never to be. And about whom, only just the other morning, I woke up thinking again. With such an intensity that it actually frightened me. And which taught me one thing – that the numbed platinum anaesthesia which one has appropriated from mimicking the orb-heads – it can never, at any time, be taken for granted. That is a lesson I learned from that experience.

I had been downtown that morning, I remember, just rambling about a little – rather aimlessly, I have to admit, and was making my way across the Plaza back towards the apartment. Where Vesna, or so I presumed, was preparing my dinner, as usual. When, quite unexpectedly, I found myself standing in the middle of an old-fashioned farmers' market. Which jolted me, I have to say. For I hadn't been expecting to encounter such a thing. I hadn't even thought they were in existence any longer.

But they were – and the effect this one now exerted upon me was deeply disconcerting, frighteningly so. For, almost immediately, I experienced an unsettling sensation consuming my entire body, as certain old familiar undermining sentiments began – with resolute, incremental authority – to assert themselves. Resulting, within a matter of mere seconds – astoundingly, as I stood there on the concrete flags – in my experiencing, with shocking clarity, the apprehension that somehow I had been returned to the small winding streets and roadways of the old Cullymore. To the cramped rooms of a poky little farmhouse called the Nook, and to the steamy ash pits and back yards of Wattles Lane. With the phut-phut of my Massey Ferguson 35 stuttering along the rutted tracks and gravelled lanes.

But none of that had I, at least up until that point, considered unmanageable. That did not become an issue until, out of the corner of my eye, I caught a sudden glimpse of a number of tower-stacked cardboard trays – all of which were neatly arranged in rows, some flecked with hens' droppings, others perfectly polished, mirror-smooth. And all ever so methodically lined up in columns. The thought came unbidden, as a volt of electricity shot down my spine. As, illogically, I perceived them fearfully crying:

– *Help us. Please help us!*

Before eventually retreating to a terrifying muteness.

– This is how it is, this is our lot for ever, they seemed, almost bashfully, to peal.

Then I became aware of the montage of voices: a ragged cacophony sounding close by. Muffled to such a degree that there was only a small number of them I could accurately identify. But all of them, without exception, were of the old town. I could hear Wee Dimpie McCool laughing, quite audibly.

And then Lady Thornton.

– He's my boy, she said, he's my boy and for your information I'm not a whore.

Then I saw Henry – standing before the drawing-room fire, as stern and grave and judicious as ever. But – and this was what truly shocked me – when he turned his expression had altered. Indeed, even more unexpectedly, his countenance now actually bore no expression at all. It was quite blank – round and empty as a perfectly polished egg. Something you expected in the new world – not the old.

Even yet, the disparate hubbub gave no indication of abating: in fact, rose in volume, becoming like a frenetic beating of wings.

All I can remember is a woman approaching – regarding me with no expression of any kind. Balloon-head, I thought, go away, please.

I endeavoured to betray no evidence of the gravity of my inner turmoil. As I respectfully replied, in the tones of an automaton:

172

– I'm fine thank you, ma'am. Thank you for your concern.

In the circumstances, I would be inclined to say, it was a creditable performance. Then, with my heart racing, I gazed across the Plaza and found them there, convened as always, passing the wine robotically across the table. It ought to have been, as before, reassuring – predictable, comforting in its uniformity. But it wasn't. It was anything but. Then I turned towards the other side of the square. On the screen of the plasma as it rotated above the courthouse, an image of Dolores McCausland was now being relayed, but upon her shoulders was Marcus Otoyo's head: sanctified, silent – raising his young eyes up to heaven.

It was only when I turned the corner that the violent trembling began anew. And I found myself fleeing in haste from a truly ghastly consideration – that, at any moment, a zig-zag fissure would open up inside me, making its way with a cruel, methodical determination down the very centre of my being. With devastating intent, preparing to release an overwhelming tumult of lava. And that perhaps which I feared more than anything – a tidal wave of sentiment and emotion.

A bead of perspiration dropped on to the back of my hand – as I saw my mother, real as I'd ever seen her – Lady Thornton's form gathering slowly before me, now sitting by the window of the Manor reading to Little Tristram.

– Tristram dear, would you like a little poem? I heard her say, as clearly as if she'd been standing right beside me.

– Of course you would, she said, and gently turned the pages, smiling.

'Escape at Bedtime' was the poem she was reading. Of course it was. It had to be. As Tristram sucked his thumb, swaying in her lap to the movement of her words.

– It's mine! I heard the shrill cry escape my lips. Don't read it to him, Mama! Fuck him, Little Tristram – little Protestant bastard!

The traffic was roaring past now, with the concrete flyover above the Plaza almost attaining the fluidity of liquorice, swooping above my head and looping back on itself as Lady Thornton continued to read:

> – *They saw me at last and they chased me with cries,*
> *And they soon had me packed into bed,*
> *But the glory kept shining and bright in my eyes,*
> *And the stars going round in my head.*

As I cradled my head in the crook of my elbow, the scene began to become even more realistic than I felt I could humanly bear: overhead I could see Cassiopeia and beside that constellation – Orion.

Then: *the star of the sailor,* and *Mars.*

Just as they would have been on that fateful night in 1940. When the big-band music they'd been playing in the Manor had at last begun to ebb and my father Stanislaus Carberry, a burly accountant with the physique of a labourer, calmly led my mother out into Thornton's barn, stroking her hair and whispering intimately into her ear. Holding her roughly amidst the haybales as he asked her what was it about Protestants, what was the truth about the mystery of

Protestants, why were they so near and yet so far away and distant or was that, in fact, the case with all human beings? Adjacent but separated – by an abyss.

– What is the mystery of human beings, my dearest fragrant honey, give us a kiss there, Lady Thornton, ah the Catholic cock and the Protestant lace.

How had she answered Stanislaus Carberry that night, I had often wondered – so many times. What reply could she have made on that eventful, moonlit wartime night, when my father, pausing for a moment to expel some wind, had proceeded to administer a 'rub of the relic', bestowing on his son the sacred gift of human life, in the darkness of a haggard all those long years before.

But it is well over eighteen months now since that regrettable episode in the farmers' market. And I haven't returned to the vicinity since. I don't even know if it's still held there or not. I just don't bother going, that's all. And whenever I'm going into the centre of Cullymore East, to buy a paper or whatever, I always make sure to take the long way round. Round by the Aldi supermarket, in fact – not all that far from the original Wattles Lane. All of which has long since been levelled. It's an office block now belonging to some consortium or other and leads directly to the Otaka restaurant.

The truth was that, before she met me, Vesna had actually worked as a cleaner there in the evenings. So she'd saved a little, and with the bit of money I'd put away over the years – and of course, like every other citizen my age, I am in receipt of an old-age pension – we're financially secure in Happy Club apartments.

After my 'little turn' in the farmers' market, I became extremely concerned that that wonderful *numbness*, that benign *sterility* which had sustained me for so long was on the verge of fragmenting, if not disappearing for ever. How could it have happened? I kept asking myself. A few trays of eggs, I fruitlessly complained, it's uh-uh-uh-absurd, so it is!

However, this much I knew – I never wanted it to happen again. I knew I couldn't afford to let it. For once that zigzag fissure appeared: it had the potential to grow with a quite bewildering but fiercely destructive speed. But, thankfully, as I say, all of that is over now, and I can safely say we won't be witnessing a recurrence.

Thus the Happy Club opens up every night, with Vesna resting there, propped up on her lacy pillows, as her husband hums Tony Bennett or Karen Carpenter. Musing:

– My Croatian love. *We've only just begun*, ha ha.

The truth being, really, that to all intents and purposes we have more or less bidden goodbye to the club called Mood Indigo for ever. For, as Paul Newman once remarked of his own wife Joanne Woodward, why eat hamburger when you've steak at home. Vesna laughs whenever I say that. But there can be no mistaking the fact that she feels complimented. As I trace my finger along her pale-blue lips, placing little kisses all along her powder-white arms. Counting the minutes until it's time – for the moon to come out and the golden treasury to be read.

– 'Escape at Bedtime' in our Happy Club home, I'll say to her, fixing us both a nice daiquiri.

Although, having said that our days in the club most likely are numbered, only two nights ago I dropped into Mood Indigo. The minute I appeared Mike Corcoran shouting out:

– Ah, there he is, the very man I was looking for, Pops McCool – you're just in time to give me a hand.

He gave me the job of putting up a few decorations, for they were throwing a party in honour of George Best – apparently it was the fortieth anniversary of the game against Benfica.

– Hand me up those pennants there, Pops, come on now, lad, shake a leg – there's work to be done! he laughed, climbing a stepladder with a red flag clenched between his teeth. As I reeled in a line of the Man. United triangles.

By the time we were finished the place was a red-and-white 'United' wonderland. They had really gone to town on the Georgie stuff too – all of it adding to the 'retro' feel, which is part and parcel of the whole Mood Indigo attraction, the 'sixties vibe', as the proprietor calls it. With coloured advertisements pasted all over the walls, including everything from *World Cup Willie* to chewing gum to cigarettes and Chevrolet cars. They had done up behind the bar, too – it was a riot. A veritable Day-Glo kitsch montage: with Jackie Onassis in her knee-length black, smiling over at Sean Connery playing James Bond in *Dr No*.

After we'd finished stringing up the pennants, I sat drinking with Mike, just laughing and joking and chatting away about old times. And although I kept insisting that I couldn't remain long, that Vesna was on her own back at the apartment, he succeeded, as usual, in persuading me to stay – to listen to a couple of tunes from the band. And I was glad that I did, for, at my request, they played a lot of my favourites – including 'No Milk Today', 'Goodnight Midnight' and 'Come Back and Shake Me', Clodagh Rodgers' two greatest hits.

I was in my element, I have to say, sitting by the window, in my favourite place. Watching the go-go girls in their wet-look boots, mischievously teasing Fat Curly the comedian.

– *Och come on, me auld muckers! Surely youse have to laugh!* he snorted as he did a vaudeville version of the twist, with the girl scissoring her legs around Fat Curly's waist, before saying goodbye as Mike and the Chordettes started up anew.

There were spot prizes after a while and one of the highlights was their cover of 'Sugar, Sugar', the theme by the Archies, if you recall.

Outshone, however, as always, by:

– *I am the Eggmah! I am the Walnut!*

I can hardly believe it myself whenever I reflect on what happened after that. It's mind-blowing, really – even to think about.

For, with absolutely no warning of any kind, bold as brass, who should come walking out in front of the stage, wiggling her hips without so much as a care in the world? *Lulu*, if you don't mind – arguably the finest female singer, bar none, of the sixties. And whose hits included 'I'm a Tiger', 'The Boat That I Row' – not omitting, of course, the quite unforgettable 'To Sir With Love', from the 1969 movie of the same name – with Sidney Poitier. Our visitor was sporting an Alice band and had her sparkling ginger hair turned up at the bottom in that absolutely adorable little sixties cutesy way.

Before seating herself down right at the end of the stage, dangling her legs over the edge and looking up with those lovely dimples and smoothing her black-hooped orange miniskirt beneath her bottom. Just relaxing there comfortably, taking in everything that was going around, in that lovely big-eyed happy way of hers. It was at that point I realised just how far I had actually come. How far I had actually travelled – psychologically, I mean. And I felt proud, really. How could I not?

You'll often see Lulu on the TV these days – on daytime chat shows and the like, discussing her pop career and what it had been like to grow up in the rough-and-tumble Glasgow of the post-war era. And yes, her voice is as good as ever it was. Every bit as good. Relaxing there now, she didn't seem a day over sixteen, the age she would have been when 'Boom Bang A Bang' had been a hit. Or, as my wife would have it, 'Boom Bank A Bank'!

And which the young singer had actually taken to Eurovision glory.

Ironically, a fact which had not escaped me as I saw her waltzing onstage, Lulu's movie *To Sir With Love* had been showing in the Magnet cinema in Cullymore on the night before *The Soul's Ascent* was due to play in the cathedral. It had moved me a little, recalling that detail, and for a moment or two I diverted my attention from the vital, big-eyed Scottish vocalist, easing my handkerchief from my breast pocket as I dabbed a small tear or two away.

Before returning my attentions to her – after strenuous efforts, at last attracting her attention. A delightful little ripple of pleasure running through me as I watched her pushing her little tiny fists up to her face, chuckling impishly in that girlish way – clearly gratified by the recognition.

– Peter Wyngarde at milady's service, I joked – and I could see she was getting a great kick out of it.

Peter Wyngarde, of course, being the suave-talking English buccaneer who played the part of the secret agent Jason King in *Department S.*

But that had just been a laugh, our little joke – and all the way through, subsequently, I remained as cool as a breeze. Before turning away at last, singing along with Mike and the rest of the Chordettes – effortless, nonplussed: easy come, easy go.

Talk about coming a long way. I obviously had and what was more, I knew it. For, in any other circumstances, especially after the bitter row I'd had with Vesna before coming out, even the slightest glimpse of Lulu like that – I mean she couldn't have been more than nine inches in height, about the size of the average milk bottle I would say

– who knows what effect it might have had on my equilibrium? But not now. And, as far as I was concerned, that could only point to one thing. One's essential, and indeed laudable, rock-solid stability.

I had only just arrived in that morning – after that business in the farmers' market, I mean. And being quite shaken, was obviously in no mood for altercations, serious or otherwise. Finding my wife, still as yet oblivious of my presence, talking in a low voice on the telephone: long-distance, evidently. Conversing with her sister, I surmised. Unless, of course, that too would turn out to be yet another self-serving fabrication.

– I very worried, Carla, I heard her say. So strange. The way he look at me sometimes. I get frighten.

As soon as she saw me she put the phone down.

– Darlink! she said.

– Huh-who was that on the phone just now, huh-who were you talking to? I asked her – with impressive detachment and coolness, even if I say so myself.

But, somehow, comparatively rigorous as I was, I couldn't seem to sustainedly marshal my thoughts. And my mind, maddeningly, kept returning to the stacked cardboard trays. And I kept on hearing – or thought I was hearing – that mute, collective cry: *Please help us!* I would think then of mouths as they opened and closed. But then I remembered – they didn't have any mouths. I stood there in the lounge of our apartment, with Vesna standing shivering on the landing directly above.

I couldn't stop myself staring at the wall directly behind her – where a hair-thin crack had, cruelly, already begun to form. A spiderline gradually appearing in the paintwork, oozing out of it now a glutinous amber fluid: the confluence of self-pity and sentiment, memory's lava.

It soon became apparent that if I didn't act decisively – the only outcome was to become entirely overwhelmed. For, in a matter of mere seconds, I knew, the dread aperture would have fatally widened – exponentially. Exposing, in vivid detail, a bitterly taunting tableau, a hideously parodic, grotesque assembly. Depicting the following, unfailingly, I already could sense it:

Little Tristram standing behind the high French windows, staring out – but not impassively. Standing there smirking – lofty, incurious. Blurred, sort of disfigured by the descending rivulets of streaming rain.

– Hello, Christopher my half-brother, I heard him say. Are you not coming in? Or are you not permitted? What a pity.

I flinched, covering my face with my hands.

– Hello, I'm Stan, I heard another, deeper voice say. Yes, I'm Stanislaus Carberry – you'd probably remember me, a burly accountant who looks like a labourer. I rode your mother, C.J. Slipped her a length of pipe, as the boys used to say. Gave her a bit of a dart, oh aye. They'll talk about mysteries, Christy. Mystery this and mystery that. But there's no fucking mystery. They're just like us, with the very same fears. They're just better at covering it up, that's all, and it's money and class that helps them to do it. There was no mystery the night she begged me to take her to the barn. You're far warmer than Henry'll ever be, she said. Oh how I wish I could run away with you. I like Catholics – they know how to live. Living with Thornton – you make love to a statue. I love you, Stan. Take me away. Take me away with you, Stanislaus Carberry. Not so mysterious, is it, sonny? The Protestant fanny – why, boys, it opened wide. One wee tickle and, boys, but the Proddy, didn't she go and let out the sacred light – after Carberry breached the walls of the city, after he tore the fucking gates down.

He looked at me before turning away: shrugging, unfazed.

Then I heard it – ever so softly at first, the first fragile notes of the hymn beginning to rise and converge:

> – *Abide with me; fast falls the eventide:*
> *The darkness deepens; Lord with me abide.*

As always, there was the same strange, ethereal, beguiling beauty and I found myself helplessly caught up in it – quite lost. As, paradoxically, in that tiny fleeting second it seemed that, even yet, happiness might be within my grasp.

But then I opened my eyes and saw him. I could not believe it – standing there, directly in front of me, just as he had been when we met on the street – Marcus Otoyo. In the very position where Vesna had been, directly above me. Attired in the girdled brown garb of Martin de Porres, he might have been on the verge of addressing a congregation.

Where had he come from, I asked myself.

Illogical though it might seem, I somehow succeeded in persuading myself that Vesna had for some reason shed all her clothes and forced herself into this somewhat shapeless and coarse brown Capuchin-style outfit. She was holding a missal and looking up, smiling, contriving an attitude of beatified rapture.

I began to get the joke at last as I snapped my fingers and gave my thigh a smack, beginning to appreciate the hilarity of the situation.

– Ha ha! I laughed. Vesna! Yeah, Stevie Wonder. You got the joke. You made it your business to find out who he was. Well, I have to say that I'm pretty impressed! The joke's on poor old Christy now!

I laughed again, doing a little dance. And said:

– Oh Vesna baby, you for sure are outasite! A real gone kookie, that's no lie!

I even sang a little snatch of the song:

– *My Cherie Amour, distant as the Milky Way!*

But the longer 'she' stood there – unsmiling, almost grim – the more it became apparent that, regrettably, in fact, it wasn't Vesna. Certainly it might have been her in the beginning. But, whatever the likelihood of that – it certainly wasn't the case now. I would have given anything to make him like the others – to turn him into Lulu, Herb Alpert or Mukti. To make him too a mere six or nine inches high. The size of a milk bottle, or even a table-leg – so that he mightn't represent the same threat as he did now.

But he wasn't, you see. He wasn't the height of a table-leg, I'm afraid. No, unlike all the others, Marcus Otoyo was every bit as large as I remembered him in life. Standing there, smiling, haughtily gazing down at me – casually adjusting his Foster Grant sunglasses. So cool I might not have even been in the room – as his jaws rotated and, unflappably, he continued to chew his gum.

Yes, chewing that gum, to be brutally frank about it, as if I had never existed at all. But what happened next I found even more difficult to come to terms with. As, without any indication or warning at all, he parted his lips, opened his mouth and began to sing. With his eyes uplifted and his dusky hands folded. Hardly even aware of what I was doing, already I had found myself falling to my knees, unconsciously apprehending myself as some crusader of old, a soldier of antiquity – exhausted and humbled, crouched in homage outside the gates of a sacred, shining city.

– *At last I have reached it*, I could hear my voice, clear as a bell, extolling. *This city of sapphire where abide the lost tribes.*

As Marcus Otoyo's voice sailed out across the landing, approaching a crescendo – pealing, it seemed, in the hot desert sun, borne upon it the echo of forgotten trumpets, now resounding in glory across the ramparts of history:

– *Jerusalem! Jerusalem! Hosanna, hosanna, lift up your gates and sing!*

As the minarets flickered beyond the high stone walls, the Byzantine towers gleaming as then at last it came: the robust falsetto of a vast, massed choir. Rending, it seemed, the very roof of heaven itself, booming above me in the livid sunset:

– *Hosanna in the highest! Hosanna to our King!*

With his rich voice proceeding sonorously – exactly as it had done on the steps of the high altar during the play's performance, when he had surpassed himself in his role as Blessed Martin as he continued:

– *In the holy place of love*, he continued, *the altar was heaped with fragrant masses of flowers: and as I prayed there, methought I saw the gorgeous crimson piles of glory in the west. Where a cloud floated across the western heaven, like a seraph's wing in its flaming beauty. Far beyond that hilltop city of the Bible where they had placed them, God's blooms. White flowers that were as clear and silent as my own soul, as I swooned and prepared for the descent of my last end.*

When I looked again, Marcus Otoyo had disappeared, with nothing remaining now but the thin, cowed figure of my wife staring fearfully through the fencing of the banisters. So pale, in fact, that I thought her quite beautiful. And told her so. As I slowly began my ascent of the stairs.

– Vuh-Vesna, I said, as I stroked her cheek, Vesna. I want us both to be together for ever. Together for ever in the city of love. In our own sacred home, where the gates will remain closed to the outside world for ever. And where but we too, as eternal lovers, shall reside.

I paused and looked away. Then I turned, and once more stroked her cheek.

– Do you agree to that, Vesna? Duh-duh-do you, my precious?

She choked and kind of stammered, but didn't really give a response that was satisfactory.

21   To Sir With Love

As I never tire of repeating to my beloved, even the most unremarkable events contain the potential to yield the most rewarding of life's pleasures.

– For example, Vesna, I will often remark – particularly if I am in the process of daubing her black eyelashes with this tiny little mascara brush, or buttoning her dress up at the back – how consistent is the satisfaction these small, otherwise seemingly insignificant mementos of ours continue to give us?

And which is why they are so much a part – an essential part – of our lives here in the Happy Club. All these little bits and pieces, so lovingly collected over the years: the numerous Carpenters albums, ancient singles by Herman's Hermits – all lying randomly scattered about the club – amidst, of course, the other debris, namely all the empty Martini bottles as well as who knows how many crushed packets of Peter Stuyvesants. Then there are the other – even more precious – artefacts. Such as the gilt-framed photo of Ethel Baird, which proudly adorns the mantelpiece. And which, shamefully, I'm forced to admit, I illicitly removed from her house that day. An act I'm not particularly proud of, I have to say.

But I simply couldn't resist it. Depicting as it does those two remarkable women – Ethel Baird and my mother Lady Thornton, smiling in her girlish collar with its delicate edging of smooth seed pearls. Standing beside a baby grand piano one sunny autumn day long ago, in the grounds of Thornton Manor, singing hymns on the lawn. And in which they look every inch the Protestant ladies, in their hats and gloves and perms, with husband Henry standing stiffly behind. As if to say: *However grudgingly, I must say, I do approve.*

For Marcus too, of course, Ethel never had anything but the highest of praise.

– I have never encountered such – such *honesty of feeling*, I remember her remarking, a quality particularly in evidence whenever he sings 'The Holy City' for me, that lovely old standard by Weatherly and Adams. Far and away the finest pupil I think I have ever taught, sweet Marcus Otoyo. The town of Cullymore should be so proud.

I'd watch him going in, parking the Massey out of sight across the street. Thinking of him inside the parlour, fingering the notes of 'The Holy City' on Ethel Baird's old walnut upright. At that time, it has to be emphasised, he had never demonstrated anything but the most exquisite manners towards me. In fact, was almost unbearably cour-teous. Sometimes, while he was waiting for Ethel to open the door, I could see him busying himself combing those tight corkscrew curls. And it would always seem as if time had stopped, as if this was a crystallised moment in history for us, with no past, no future – just this singular, light-flickering instant, sandwiched between twin unfathomable eternities.

The week before the performance was due to take place in the cathedral I became aware that he had started visiting Ethel's on a daily basis. In the end I just decided to leave the tractor behind. And just stand there in the alleyway, withdrawing discreetly into the shadows, imagining that the recital was being conducted solely for my benefit. It was just a harmless illusion, that's all, with his pristine voice sailing through the opening of the raised sash window, wafting out into the drab surroundings, transforming the world through a heart-stirring alchemy.

As I clasped *A Portrait* in my two folded hands, elevating my eyes towards the dome of the sky, where, lit by the sun in unclouded splendour, I might have apprehended the towers and pinnacles of the holy city, distantly gleaming by the side of a tideless sea.

– O Zion, I prayed, put on thy beautiful garments – and be as a bride adorned for her husband.

I knew Sidney Poitier was the star of the Hollywood film *To Sir With Love* but that was pretty much all I knew. I had finished up unexpectedly early that evening, I remember, and had been treating myself to a few pleasant glasses in the Good Times, before heading to 'the pictures', as they used to call them in Cullymore.

So it would have been about seven-thirty or eight when I finally made it up to the Magnet. I know that it might be possible to infer, considering my already established patterns of behaviour at the time, that I had spent all that evening following, effectively shadowing, Marcus Otoyo. That maybe, in fact, I had planned the whole thing, unable to help myself. But that really isn't true – it was just by chance that he happened to be at the pictures. Black though he might have been himself, I would have been very surprised if he had ever heard of Sidney Poitier. So I am sure he just happened, more or less on a whim, to go to the cinema. Yes, the whole thing had happened completely by accident. Of course it had. But of course. I'm certain of that. Yes. Pointless thinking otherwise.

But I had got such a shock, I remember, when I saw him. I was sure that he'd be at home, availing himself of what little time remained for the purpose of assiduously consolidating his lines.

A whole three weeks had now elapsed since the night of the disastrous Beachcomber Affair.

I had been inside the cinema no more than five minutes when I felt the hairs bristling on the back of my neck. In fact, my skin was beginning to crawl. As I realised, with a kind of delicious horror, that he was seated almost directly below me, in the stalls. Like any ordinary, impishly confrontational youth, as I realise now, defiantly draped across the padded upholstery. With a cigarette – I have to confess to being somewhat shocked, although I possessed no such authority – sullenly suspended from his lips. I recalled a line from a classical anthology I had been perusing recently in the library, and which had read: *in whose luxuriant confines the desultory convivialists habitually exhibit themselves.*

He was unaccompanied, lolling there casually, uninterested, alone – flicking his cigarette with a kind of awkward, sullen boredom. He was wearing his braided bottle-green blazer. Now and then, in the projection beam, I would see his high glossy forehead suddenly appear. Then I heard him yawn and my heart began to race. As the curtains parted and, unbidden, once more the hymn began its ascent in my mind:

– *Hosanna!* I heard, and trembled as I did do. *Hosanna to your King!*

As I fled in anxiety from the incipient crash of the mighty brass cymbals, the soaring crescendo of imagined choral voices. My attention, happily, and with incommunicable relief, being unexpectedly diverted by the basso profundo of the onscreen commentator, as a sprightly advert for Blue Band commanded attention in the crackling, dusty darkness.

– *It's the margarine the whole country is talking about – soft and spreadable, all the way from the USA!*

The film had told the story of a black American teacher relocated to the East End of London. But of its substance I don't recall a great deal. All I can remember, in any detail worth talking about, is the presentation finally coming to an end. And standing right beside me, as we exited – Marcus Otoyo.

– Whuh-whuh-what did you think of it, Marcus? I stammered. Whuh-what did you think of Sidney Poitier? Some negro actors can be very good, can't they?

I wasn't even aware of the fact that I had spoken.

He smiled thinly, as he regarded me with some curiosity. Before responding:

– Could be. If you say so.

Yes, that was what Marcus Otoyo said that night, on an otherwise quite unremarkable summer night in 1969, three weeks after the Beachcomber Affair. Yes, three weeks after the Butlin's catastrophe. As the credits rolled on *To Sir With Love*, with Lulu's voice now belting out, fortissimo, rising to its zenith as the swaying velvet curtains closed.

The following day, which of course was the actual date of the performance, I had spent the whole morning arguing violently with myself. As to whether I ought to attend *The Soul's Ascent* or not. I had been so overwhelmed by our conversation in the cinema the night before that my ears were still burning, out of a not unreasonable sense of shame. How could I have gone and said such a stupid thing, I persistently chastised myself. In the end, I made the only decision I could. Even if, to this very day, I still wish I hadn't.

For nothing had prepared me – not even Ethel Baird's unqualified praise, the laudatory rumours I'd been hearing around the town – for the unmatched power of the boy's prodigious delivery. Of the world-famous hymn by Stephen Adams and Frederick Weatherly.

– 'The Holy City', intoned Canon Burgess, stepping aside as he introduced Marcus. Our Blessed Martin de Porres.

The boy's eyes, mindful of his duties as a performer and out of respect for the work of the authors, were already tightly shut.

It would have been better if I had vacated the cathedral there and then. With an alacrity similar to that displayed in the Beachcomber Bar the night of 'the affair'. When I had quit the building and not bothered to return. Yes, I ought to have instantly removed myself from that cathedral. I didn't, however. I couldn't find the strength within me to do so. Like everyone else, I was stirringly captivated.

The interior was flooded by a dull scarlet light that filtered through the lowered blinds and the rustle of pamphlet pages ebbed and swelled like a sweetly hushing wave. Which acted as a counterpoint to the magisterial chords of the pipe organ in the gallery as the first few notes came from his thick, parted lips:

– *Last night I lay a-sleeping, there came a dream so fair,*
I stood in old Jerusalem beside the temple there.
I heard the children singing and ever as they sang
Methought the voice of angels from heaven in answer rang,
Methought the voice of angels from heaven in answer rang –

In a twist of serpentine purple, the incense continued twining upwards as the pendulous silver thurible swung, temporarily obscuring the boy's darkly shining countenance, so overcome with emotion that his cheeks too were stained silver by his tears. As he gestured expansively before an altar heaped with blossoms. White flowers that

194

were clear and silent as his soul, a soul as radiant as the Eucharist itself.

– Jerusalem! Jerusalem! Lift up your gates and sing!
Hosanna in the highest! Hosanna to your King!

As I bowed my head, my soul irrevocably snared, held for ever in abject bondage. But, paradoxically, also finding its release. For I had never experienced anything quite like this: gone now were the confusions, the cumulative assaults of fallen hope and wounded pride. And in their place, an inexpressible ecstasy.

Truly glorious.

For that simple reason – I still remained in a state of *excelsis* – I decided afterwards to make it my business to locate Dolly. Who did her shopping late, in the Five Star. Taking such a decision in itself was quite remarkable – an indication in itself of just how far weakness and timidity had fallen from me.

Thus, on the very dot of five o'clock, I found myself striding into the Five Star supermarket, and, as luck would have it, within seconds, happening upon the lady in question. And who looked, I have to say, even more beautiful than ever on this occasion.

I made it my business to engage her immediately in conversation. I couldn't stop talking, actually, such was the effect the performance had exerted. I don't think I had even switched off the engine of the Massey. I think, perhaps, that, in retrospect, I may have made her uneasy – displaying such an effusive and quite forthright manner. I mean it's not what Protestants expect or tend to be comfortable with. But then Dolly had always been different, I persuaded myself. Always had been. A Protestant in a league of her own – that was how I'd always thought of Dolores McCausland. And why I felt certain that, given a moment or two, she would come round.

Which is the reason I found myself extremely startled, very taken aback indeed, when I heard her announce, very sharply, that she intended leaving town. Was packing her bags the following Thursday, in fact.

As soon as I heard her say it, almost immediately I found myself beginning to regret the cold detachment and indifference that had become a part of our relations towards the end. And couldn't stop thinking of all the fun we'd had in the beginning – all those nights in the Mayflower and the Good Times, singing and dancing: and how I was sad that it hadn't worked out.

For, at the back of it all, I think that Dolores had genuinely expected – had been confident, in fact – that she and I would eventually become engaged. But it was not to be. I set my teeth and summoned what reserves of self-possession remained, but could sense the commingling forces of confused ardour and regret beginning to converge. Doing my best to simultaneously evade and deny them, tapping my foot as I leaned against the brass checkout rail:

– Yes, the great Summer of Love, it now draws to a close. Will you ever forget it – the Beatles, the Animals, Eric Burdon! *In the dirty old part of the city, where the sun refuse to shine! Yeah!*

– It's lovely to meet you, she said, but I really now must be going.

– Is it because of the letter? I asked.

– That's not the only thing, she said. The letter was one thing . . .

– What else could there be?

– Maybe you should ask your little black friend, she said bitterly.

It was only later that I was to learn that some difficulty had developed between Dolores and Marcus's mother. Who had discovered something she did not quite appreciate about her lodger and former friend. Had not liked at all what she had discovered, regarding certain unwholesome affections between Dolly Mixtures and her son. And, like any mother, did not find herself disposed to laying the blaming on the boy.

– Please, Dolly! Don't go yet! I implored her.

She gathered up her belongings and groceries, refusing to acknowledge me as I accompanied her towards the exit.

– Did you ever think of seeing someone? she said then, turning abruptly – and these were to be her parting words to me, as she added:

– It might be a good idea before you start deceiving other people, Christopher.

– But it was you! You did it with him – that night in Butlin's!

– You know what I'm talking about, now if you don't mind I have to go.

And as I watched her walking down the road – suddenly somehow seeming much older, with her sheepskin ill-fitting

197

and her headscarf somewhat drab – I shook my head and mused, regretfully: Yes, she had been beautiful, my Dolores.

And maybe in another universe the two of us could have made it – lived a fulfilled and contented life as Mr and Mrs Christopher Thornton. With the ceremony being performed by both a vicar and a Catholic priest – just to keep all sides happy, as they say. How beautiful that might have been, I considered. But now, for ever – to remain a mystery.

In any case, as I knew only too well, something even more beautiful had happened. In a Catholic cathedral that very day. How could I have been so fortunate? I struck my breast in gratitude, reproaching myself for former failings and shortcomings of belief.

Then I drove the Massey out to the Nook, chanting 'The Holy City' all the way there. Before searching for and finding the single item that I loved more than anything in the world. I was like a kid on Christmas morning, for heaven's sake, preparing to wrap it up in brown paper, pausing for a moment to admire its metallic cover, the gold-leaf lettering arched above its many water-coloured wonders – including the clear crystal fountain, the two looping bluebirds and the fantailing sprinkle of silver, nightfalling stars. *A Child's Garden of Verses by Robert Louis Stevenson*, its title read. Kissing the cover and tucking it excitedly underneath my arm, before heading, immediately, back into town.

22 In the Holy of Holies

The new Novotel in the centre of Cullymore East is one of a number which have been constructed in recent times and I have only just been reading that plans are already afoot to begin work on yet another thousand-room, conference-hosting establishment – a Radisson, this time, I believe. Which, it has been proposed, will be sited in the centre of the Plaza, not far in fact from the place where Green Shield Stamps used to be.

Vesna and I used to go to the Novotel every weekend. That is to say before what you might call the 'final betrayal'. To which I'd been alerted by the *Perfidia* website. Which, as a matter of course, cautioned all spouses, without exception, against complacency. *Common manifestations of deceit. Adultery – signs to look out for*, the masthead read.

I used to enjoy it there in the Novotel, though, with Vesna touching my hand as we relaxed there together, sipping a drink or taking afternoon tea perhaps. As the noiseless glass lift elevated and descended, with the pearly disc of the receptionist's head bobbing so gently.

The manager liked to see us coming in and generally made it his business to join us. Just for a little while to ensure that we were comfortable. He is a man in his forties, customarily attired in a sharp pinstripe suit, with a high collar and tie and an oval face which seems softer, a little less featureless than many of the others. I used always to listen dutifully to his dithering and fussing and can only hope that my nods were both appropriate and convincing. He still asks about her, obviously, whenever he happens to see me. So I just trot out the usual fluff about Dubrovnik.

– Ah, she's gone to see Mama, he smiles, his egghead unmoving like a great massive dot.

Featureless, however, though his countenance might have been, it was plain to me quite early on that the Eggman hotelier harboured certain affections for Vesna from Dubrovnik, touching her, I noticed, in a manner quite inappropriate at times. Not in a sexually intimate way – just little glancing brushes along her arm or the back of her hand.

Not that I blame him. Indeed it would be churlish not to say childish of me to do so – especially whenever Vesna was sporting one of her more figure-hugging numbers. She had come a long way now from her old-fashioned image, when she looked like someone thirty years out of date, who ought to have been strumming a stupid guitar, crooning 'Moon Shadow' or some comparable drivel. She even had a photo of herself looking like that, with a bunch of her friends sitting with guitars near a beach hut somewhere, waving at the camera in their bikinis and blue jeans as if to announce: Our songs will save the world, iss good?

* * *

The Mood Indigo Club, as it happens, is actually making a fortune now, or so I heard from Mike when I met him recently. Thanks to the enduring popularity of the sixties 'retro' boom. The Chordettes, as a result, having decided to completely remodel themselves, dropping the Las Vegas image altogether, he tells me. Yes, the wide lapels, frilled shirts and gold chains have all, apparently, gone. With yachting blazers and neat grey slacks now the order of the day, a trend best decribed, perhaps, as 'grandpa chic'. He asked me in for a Martini and I agreed, as it slipped down finding myself returning to that final day in Cullymore. When I made my way across the fields, along the railway track that led to their little restored greenhouse.

This was the evening of 'the great performance', a mere few hours after Marcus Otoyo had taken the town by storm, delivering a rendition of 'The Holy City' that would be talked about years hence in the town. Which was the reason, of course, that I'd waited in the main street for an opportunity to present to him the golden treasury, and to congratulate him on a truly wonderful performance. I'd seen it, really, as a token of gratitude. Simply wanted to display my appreciation. Of his bountiful talents and achievements.

That it didn't work out is unfortunate, that's all. It didn't happen, and there isn't really a lot more you can say. And, in a way, it was nobody's fault. Although I did probably come across as excessively enthusiastic, far too eager by half. Such an approach was almost inevitably going to embarrass a boy of his tender age. So, no matter how one views it, I had essentially been the architect of my own misfortune. And, hardly had the words even left my mouth, than I myself became aware that this was indeed the case. But in no way does it excuse my subsequent behaviour. Which was heedless, to say the least – quite callous, in fact. Maybe even unforgivable, in the eyes of some people.

There was one unfortunate individual in particular, I remember, a regular lady customer of mine, as it happened, who had made a point of calling me over – apparently she wanted to cancel the following week's egg and milk order. Explaining, quite reasonably, that she had changed her plans and was going away on holiday.

– Hello, Christopher, she'd called, signalling from across the street. I wonder could I have a wee word?

To which I had responded by laughing into her face as I sang her a verse of Herman's Hermits' popular hit:

– *No milk today, my love has gone away!*

I regret very much that that had to happen, for it left the lady in question hurt and extremely confused, to the advantage of no one. To make matters worse, I continued repeating the lyrics as I walked away, doing a little dance routine that Dolores and I had learned from the Shadows, and with which we had amused ourselves in the Mayflower of old.

It was about a mile from the town to the Holy of Holies and all the way there I kept doggedly trying – absurd as it now seems, for we were only talking about a matter of hours – to reclaim the equanimity I had known directly before the performance of *The Soul's Ascent*. How I longed to be once more the person that I had been then, a mere few hours previously. In my strenuous efforts to do so becoming so overwrought that just for one second I harboured a dark desire to become as Henry Thornton had been – for that fleeting moment inhabit his reptilian skin. For that single instant to be permitted to gain access to qualities I now yearned for: those of incuriosity, neutrality, of calculated detachment and indifference.

But it never would happen, as I knew. With my own words to Marcus Otoyo now returning – bringing a blush to my already burning cheeks:

– Muh-muh-Marcus, wuh-wuh-will you uh-appease the longings of my yuh-yuh-yearning heart? Will you, Muh-Marcus, Minor?

His reaction, I knew, would remain with me for ever. As I thought of him standing there, in the drab drizzle of the main street, pushing his tongue aggressively against his teeth, shrugging his shoulders as he fixed me with an accusatory gaze, his patient jaws ever so slowly rotating. Before, eventually, parting his lips and exclaiming:

– *Freak.*

Making my way now across the fields, past the deserted warehouses and engine sheds, along the rusted railway tracks, already in my mind all thoughts of the great sixties decade and what it had been supposed to represent in history fading in my mind and fading fast.

– A false dream! I complained bitterly, as I stumbled awkwardly over the sharp glittering chunks of shale piled up between the wooden sleepers, my eyes blinded by tears of disappointment.

A false dream constructed by advertising executives and cynical exploiters of human frailty and emotion – Billy Butlin included. It was astonishing, I thought, as, heartsick, I pressed onwards, that any right-thinking individual could ever have entertained such frivolous nonsense. The bubblegum decade, flimsy and ephemeral. But for which, I reflected, I myself was almost the perfect avatar, the very embodiment of what I was deriding. Clad as I was in my candy-striped jacket, with an absurdly large knot on my purple paisley tie, perfectly matching my enormous scalloped collar.

– Hey! I laughed, helpless, it's 1969 and all of you are welcome to the show of the decade. We present: *It's C.J.!*

Now what would that be like, I paused to wonder as I continued to sidestep the sharp chunks of shale. With xylophone arpeggios chiming in a parade of miniskirted dancers as an enormous series of giant *It's C.J.!* polystyrene letters were spectacularly unveiled as showers of multi-coloured confetti fell to the ground, the strains of the music becoming out of control as he stepped in from the wings – Marcus Otoyo in his Foster Grant sunglasses, blowing a mischievous kiss from his lace-cuffed hand.

– What a crazy guy! I laughed. He's a real gone kook!

When all of a sudden, stimulated by a glint of sunlight leaping from the stones, the loveliest little story entered my mind, like a glimpse of entirely unexpected treasure. One which I remembered in from my schooldays.

'The Golden Windows', that story was called and it told the tale of a young boy who long ago had lived in a lonely mountain valley. And who, after months of nervous apprehension, had eventually decided to make the trip across the unknown terrain of his mountain valley to investigate the mystery of the shining golden window, whose panes of amber had for so long transfixed him. To his dismay, then discovering, after he had completed his arduous journey, that the very windows he had so desired were in every conceivable way as unremarkable as those familiar from his own humble cottage. Even yet I could remember the burden of his disappointment. And I prayed that my story wouldn't end in such a fashion.

As I approached the greenhouse, already I could make out the figure of Evelyn Dooris, with her small stooped shape bent over some flowers. At first she didn't react when she saw that it was me. Standing beside her, holding the torn package, somewhat vacantly, in my hand.

– I don't know why you're here, she said, returning to her labours. There wouldn't be any eggs a-wanting here.

It was beautiful, really, that little greenhouse: the Holy of Holies. There were candles and little vases and a lovely little makeshift altar: a china bowl with primroses inside and a printed card edged in gold which read: *Blessed Martin de Porres. Petition the Pope for his canonisation.*

Evelyn's manner was curt, a trifle impatient. Eventually she turned to face me.

– Well, what have you to say? Can't you see that I'm busy? How can I help you, Mr McCool?

– No matter what Marcus Otoyo might tell you, Evelyn, it isn't true. I just wanted you to know that.

She paid me little heed: even seemed aggrieved.

– What has Marcus Otoyo got to do with me? He doesn't come out here any more. He says it's childish. He's changed, if you must know – even ignores me now when he sees me. So I don't know what you're talking about. And, to be perfectly honest, I don't really care. So, if you don't mind – I'm busy. I've things to do.

– I just want you to tell him, I began once more, taking her gently by the arm. Can't you just tell him that he misunderstood. I just wanted to give him this, that's all. That's all – there's nothing else. I hope you understand that.

She shrugged again and went back to her seedlings.

Before I knew it I had torn the package open and handed the book to her. The blue cover of the treasury shone in the sunlight: *A Child's Garden of Verses.*

– I don't want it, she said. I'll be taking away all this stuff now. I'm finished here. And I won't be coming back.

As I left the Holy of Holies that day, no matter how I might try to emulate Henry Thornton, my eyes continued to savagely burn. And it seemed that, no matter how manly and self-possessed my endeavours might have been in the beginning, ultimately I failed hopelessly in my efforts to dispatch those encroaching, overpowering odours – the aura of those perfumes, the evanescent aromas of the primroses and other blooms. Which she tended so lovingly she might have been a woman far in advance of her tender years – an experienced handmaid.

The intelligence which she had, quite indifferently, imparted:

– Marcus and I, we're not friends any more.

All the more wrenching for its glazed abstraction.

I recalled how pale she had looked as she'd said it and I was sorry for ever having gone out there at all.

23   The Eggman

What I find most rewarding about life in general, as I review them now, all sixty-seven years that have thus far been allotted to me, is that the common fear that after incidents of severe trauma and upset we might never be returned to 'normality' – that blithe, blissful state – is entirely without foundation. However understandable such a perception might be. Indeed, and for quite some considerable time, this was the conclusion I had reached myself.

I had been aware, of course, for some time that Vesna had been exhibiting certain signs of unease and discomfort. Not to put too fine a point on it, she had begun to seem very unhappy indeed. But it was only when the late-night sobbing started that I found myself becoming really seriously concerned.

– What's all this about, Vesna? I demanded to know. Are you not happy being married any more?

Receiving little satisfaction, I'm afraid, in spite of patient, tactful appeals. The result being, unfortunately, the development of a number of public confrontations. Which were extremely unpleasant, I am afraid I have to say. And which, as I put it to her plainly, simply could not be permitted to continue. A rational evaluation, which, happily, she came to understand. Or so she had insisted.

But then, of course, I wouldn't be the first husband to fall victim to credulity, certainly not where one's wife is concerned. The website I'd been accessing (*Perfidia.com*) had made specific reference to the enduringly hopeless innocence of men in this regard – how easily they are hoodwinked by wives and cheating girlfriends. However, aware of this as I might have been, at no time did it ever occur to me that Vesna would turn out to be so disappointingly *guileful*. For I really can think of no other way of putting it.

Even yet I find it hard to accept. I mean, ending your partner's life – it's not something you take lightly.

What happened was this: we'd been down in Mood Indigo and had had ourselves a rare old time. I'd even go so far as to say it was the best night we'd had down there in a year. There had been standing room only and the Chordettes had acquitted themselves magnificently, as usual. With Mike concluding the evening with a swirling virtuoso solo on the Hammond and Fat Curly bidding us all a 'hearty goodnight'. Waving his chequered hat as he called out after us as we made our departure:

– *Och come on, me auld muckers! Surely youse have to laugh!*

I hadn't seen Vesna in such good form for ages. Why, it was as if we'd never had so much as a disagreement in our lives. Which explains – at least I hope so – why I was so devastated, when eventually I discovered the blood-chilling truth.

What annoyed me more than anything was that the two of them had obviously been planning it for months. That I had made it so easy for them, in not suspecting the slightest thing. Not even when I heard the metal grate shifting and the first muffled whispers in behind the ventilation grid. The purpose of which was – to distract me, of course. And to provide Vesna with the opportunity she required. To divert my attention for those first few vital moments, when – ever so slyly – she could make her way down the stairs. With but one single motive in mind – that of committing the basest of sins.

Except, like in so many of these cases, the best-laid plans . . .

When, having established beyond doubt that the ventilation grid gave no cause for concern, I found myself, literally, stuck fast to the spot. As I realised that, not only had the bedclothes been seriously disturbed, but that Vesna, my wife, was nowhere to be seen. It was at that point I overheard the tinkle of suppressed laughter, intermittently drifting through the floorboards from downstairs. I steeled myself.

But nothing could have prepared me for the scene I was about to encounter.

I couldn't believe it when I saw Marcus Otoyo – his jaws rotating as he chatted away casually, as if he'd known her all his life. Vesna, of course, was hanging on his every word.

It soon became apparent that not a single detail of my life story was to be omitted. He was even telling her about the visit to Ethel's. Describing how I'd jammed my foot in the front door, demanding a private recital of hymns.

– Yes, he continued, the unfortunate lady, can you imagine? Sitting in her lap! A grown man wanting such a thing?

It was more than I could bear, as my knuckles whitened around my meerschaum cane.

And thus he got his just deserts. Before, tremblingly, I turned my attentions towards his associate – now crouching pitiably by the wall, imploring clemency. But it had gone too far for that. And I did not stop trouncing her with my cane until finally, regrettably, my partner was entirely lifeless.

As I'm sure you can imagine, it was an extremely painful and difficult period of our lives for both Vesna and me. But, as is always the case, in any marriage of any worth, there are very few problems which cannot, somehow, eventually be re-solved, and suffice to say that that is what happened. With no further secrets remaining in the Happy Club, and that is the way, without a doubt, it's going to stay. Why, in bed only last evening, I even read out the letter to my spouse, the 'sacred' missive to Dolores from 'her lover', the one I'd removed from her handbag that night.

– Listen to this, Vesna! I laughed heartily, snuggling up beside her, the bloody old envelope that caused all the heartache – I mean, can you believe it?

I cleared my throat and smoothed out the pages, chuck-ling a little as I read:

Love's City:

– Ariadne my beloved, my precious, how my heart aches and

longs for you these past few nights. Since last we met there have been nothing but fond thoughts of you in my mind. There are times when I fear I shall lose my reason, so intense are the feelings my soul harbours for you. I can find no name for them save those of wounded pride, fallen hope and baffled desire. I love you, Dolores – be assured of that. Yours for ever, Marcus Minor

Which was hilarious from start to finish, or so it seemed to me. Except that, when I looked up, I discovered that Vesna wasn't laughing. Instead, pale as a sheet, was pointing over towards one corner of the room. To where, beside the opened ventilation space, Little Tristram Thornton, in height no bigger than the average jam-jar, to my astonishment, was sucking his thumb and perusing his golden treasury. Before naively looking up, then shrieking like a flock of jackdaws vacating the Thornton Manor treetops:

– *C.J. Pops has been tricked again! C.J. Pops has been tricked again!*

As, in mortal dread, I turned my head towards the bed once again, finding there not Vesna Krapotnik, or anyone like her. But in her place a complete stranger, resting his chin upon a cane, eyeing me with a chill, mute poise: the stark orb of his head void – white and virginal – as perfectly formed as a consecrated bread.

212

A NOTE ON THE TYPE

The text of this book is set in Adobe Garamond. It is one of several versions of Garamond based on the designs of Claude Garamond. It is thought that Garamond based his font on Bembo, cut in 1495 by Francesco Griffo in collaboration with the Italian printer Aldus Manutius. Garamond types were first used in books printed in Paris around 1532. Many of the present-day versions of this type are based on the *Typi Academiae* of Jean Jannon, cut in Sedan in 1615.

Claude Garamond was born in Paris in 1480. He learned how to cut type from his father and by the age of fifteen he was able to fashion steel punches the size of a pica with great precision. At the age of sixty he was commissioned by King Francis I to design a Greek alphabet; for this he was given the honourable title of royal type founder. He died in 1561.

ALSO AVAILABLE BY PATRICK MCCABE:

WINTERWOOD

Once, in Kilburn, married to the sugar-lipped Catherine and sharing his daughter Immy's passion for the enchanted kingdom of Winterwood, Redmond Hatch was happy. But then infidelity, betrayal and the 'scary things' from which he would protect his daughter steal into the magic kingdom, and bad things begin to happen. Now Redmond – once little Red – prowls the barren outlands alone, haunted by the disgraced shade of Ned Strange, a fiddler and teller of tales from his home in the mountainy middle of Ireland.

✳

'A true original'
JOHN BANVILLE

'This is McCabe's greatest work …
A sustained achievement of often dazzling brilliance'
IRVINE WELSH, GUARDIAN

'A masterpiece'
OBSERVER

✳

ISBN 9 780 7475 8598 5 · PAPERBACK · £7.99

ORDER YOUR COPY: BY PHONE +44 (0)1256 302 699; BY EMAIL: DIRECT@MACMILLAN.CO.UK
DELIVERY IS USUALLY 3–5 WORKING DAYS. FREE POSTAGE AND PACKAGING FOR ORDERS OVER £20.

ONLINE: WWW.BLOOMSBURY.COM/BOOKSHOP
PRICES AND AVAILABILITY SUBJECT TO CHANGE WITHOUT NOTICE.

WWW.BLOOMSBURY.COM/PATRICKMCCABE

BLOOMSBURY